AFFIRMATION

PAGAN EYES, BOOK 4

BY

RAYNA NOIRE

Published by Sleeping Dragon

www.raynanoire.com
www.facebook.com/AuthorRaynaNoire

CHAPTER ONE

THE PROFESSOR'S VOICE bounced off the cement block walls and lab tables giving his words a brittle quality. Stella twisted around to see if any of the other students noticed, but most weren't even taking notes. Those with laptops open were either shopping or updating statuses. A chime caused her to glance at her phone. Instead of seeing a message from her co-worker, Mitch, about dying from boredom, the text was from Cameron. Her heart leapt a little when she saw his name.

Need to see you right away. Ditch class.

Besides being the resident bad boy, he was her bad boy. The thought made her smile. It lasted only a few seconds as she considered his behavior. Lately, Cam had been no treat, always demanding she do things for him, never considering she might have a life too.

Part of her wanted to jump out of her seat to see what the dark-eyed junior needed. Another part counseled her to stay. The only reason she'd made it to college was due to a merit scholarship. If she didn't keep her grades up, she'd lose the scholarship. Leaving class, especially during Dr. Engelhard's exam review, could be academic suicide.

Still, Cameron wanted her. He needed her. Quite a difference from her father, who dropped out of her life the same time he divorced her mother. His parting sally as she and her mom stood on the front lawn was, "You ruined my life." Its intended target could have been either of them, although, a search for her shot records for college uncovered her parents' marriage certificate, proving they married shortly before her birth. Other parents divorced. At least half the kids on campus came from divorced parents, but few had battled as bitterly or as publicly as hers had.

Picking up her pencil, she forced herself to concentrate on the notes on the board. Her attention wandered. Lately, it went down pathways she'd rather forget like her parents red-faced, screaming at one another, somehow unaware she was even in the house. Not only did she discover her mother got pregnant which forced her father into marriage, but she also learned her dad was no prize in the bedroom, all things she could have lived without knowing.

Her phone chimed again. Cameron. The man might be hot, but not patient. Sighing deeply, she slumped in her chair. No way around it, Cam would keep texting her until she showed.

Mitch leaned over to whisper, "I'll make you a copy of my notes. I'll bring them to you at the computer lab."

"Thanks."

Her reply, unfortunately, attracted the prof's attention. He stopped writing to stare right at her and spoke. "Some of us think this review is for my own benefit."

The few students who were actually paying attention giggled nervously.

Stella picked up her pencil and pretended to write until the prof turned back to the board, giving her a chance to escape. She gathered her notebook and phone and shoved them both in her bag. Mitch gave her a wave as she turned for the door.

The lanky male with the bad haircut had traits she wished Cam possessed. A few of the girls joked about a blind man cutting Mitch's hair. At the time, she'd said nothing, but she should have stood up for him. Mitch trained her for her computer lab job and never lost patience with her no matter how many times she had to ask him the same questions. Now, he was taking notes for her too.

The sunlight hit her as she pushed the heavy exterior door open. Her feet stumbled to a stop, her pupils adjusting to the bright light. A student behind her shoved past, jostling her a little. Voices made her step out of the way before someone else rammed her.

Wasn't that Cam near the weeping magnolia tree talking to Carlotta? The exotic Puerto Rican had most of the males on campus running into walls. The beauty not only had plenty of curves, but her accent attracted too. Stella's mother always said men loved anything new and different. At the time, she thought her mother meant cars.

Seriously, she left class for him and here he was flirting with Senorita Skank. Well, screw him. Maybe she'd just return to class and hope the prof hadn't noticed her exit. Not likely. The best she'd do was go to her room and study. Of course, she'd have to walk past Cam, unless she wanted to make a half-mile detour. No problem, she'd pretend she didn't even see them.

Don't act upset. Shouldering her backpack, she speed-walked in the direction of the couple. *Almost past,* the pain that grabbed her heart when she first saw the two of them squeezed a little tighter. Once she was in her room, she'd locate her Wiccan books. For Cameron, she'd dropped everything from her interest in Art Club to observing her Wiccan faith. Her mother had warned that men take everything but leave you with nothing. Her mother's newest obsession was the church, which seemed to demand everything too.

Cam's deep voice called after her, "Stella, wait."

His voice as warm and smooth as caramel had actually won her over initially. That and the fact that he didn't give up easy since he asked her out six times before she'd agreed. It baffled her that he wanted to go out with her. Rumors had him practically dating everyone in her dorm, but never more than once.

Realistically, he should have moved on after their first date. Maybe this was her wake-up call. Cam's hand latched onto her arm, pulling her to a stop. "What's wrong with you? You act like you didn't hear me."

The impromptu sprint ruffled his hair, making him look even sexier with his well-shaped brows arched over his brown eyes. Stella often wondered if he'd had his eyebrows shaped, but never felt like she knew him well enough to ask, despite sleeping together. He'd probably lie about it anyhow.

"Looked like you were busy. I didn't want to interrupt."

Her shoulders went up in a shrug, hoping it looked like she didn't care too much.

His brows lowered as he grinned, displaying for a moment that wicked smile that devastated feminine hearts, especially hers. Stella's ire began to melt away under the full wattage of his smile.

"You think." He shook his head as if what he was about to say was ridiculous. "I was flirting with her?"

Stella sucked in her lips wondering if she'd been hasty in her assumptions. After all, she hadn't heard what they said, even if their bodies turned toward one another, blocking out the outside world, indicated an intimate meeting. "The two of you had your heads close together. People might mistake it for flirting."

Good, she didn't say it looked like flirting. No reason for him to think she was needy and insecure, even if she was.

His laugh garnered attention from passing students she could have done without. "Please, Stella." He wrapped one arm around her shoulders and pulled her into his side before continuing. "How could you imagine such a thing when I only have eyes for you?"

The words soothed her some, but part of her pointed out that his eyes checked out the passing women too. The reassurance helped a little, but it didn't restore the euphoria from their first date. Romcom movies oversold her on the wonders of love. The rush disappeared, leaving behind irritation at the demands of a relationship. Right now, she should be taking notes for a crucial exam. People assumed she was naturally smart, but she wasn't. Studying, making flash cards and endless notes earned her the scholarship. Thank goodness, Mitch was copying notes for her, which was the behavior she'd expect from a boyfriend, but didn't get from Cameron.

The man had some type of sexual magic he did with his eyes and lips that short-circuited her rational thought process until she forgot why she was upset with him. Not happening. No way, she'd fall under the spell of his bedroom eyes now. She directed her gaze over his shoulder to where she could see dozens of students strolling the commons. Some hurried, most carried books, and a few ambled prolonging their time together in the stage of initial attraction. She remembered it well.

Before Cameron, she'd gone out in high school a little, but not much. Truthfully, she was afraid of being too attached to someone. Her goal centered on bypassing love and the accompanying devastation that happened when it ended. Her heart and a desire for companionship interfered. Cam wore her down on a night when her inability to reach Leah left her feeling unusually lonely and friendless.

Cam asked her out the first time they'd met in the campus bookstore. She'd refused, thinking he wasn't serious. Another girl at her dorm went with him instead, proving her original assumption right. Despite her full schedule and a work-study job in the computer department, she wasn't so busy she didn't notice that almost every hot girl in her dorm claimed to have gone out with Cam.

They'd usually gush about his cut body and fabulous hair, not that they ever spoke to her. She overheard them. College courses demanded more of her time than high school ever did, leaving her little time to socialize. Her mingling skills, while never stellar, grew stale with her determination to keep up her grades.

The weight of Cam's arm pulled her from her impromptu reverie. Not totally over her irritation over the romantic tryst she'd witnessed caused her to jerk away, but he tightened his hold, pulling her back to his side. A burst of chatter as students passed by quelled her initial protest. Currently, she wasn't feeling all that loving toward Cam. She could do without his arm wrapped around her, even though his gesture didn't signify much since many students walk arm in arm or with an arm wrapped around the other. Cut off from their familiar family support, the younger students often clung to each other, joking about their actions. The addition of alcohol blurred personal boundaries even more.

Cam's lips brushed her ear. "No need for jealousy since you're mine now."

The half-growled words sounded more like a threat than a romantic promise, especially when accompanied by a tight grip. No, she didn't feel the love. She wiggled her shoulders to loosen his hold without success. Not his usual behavior, which ran toward texted meeting places as opposed to actually arriving together. His public show of affection should make her happy, but instead it made her suspicious. It reminded her of the magazine article about cheating stating that the offender pours on affection hoping to cover his tracks.

"What was so important that I had to leave class?"

His arm dropped from her shoulders as he grinned. "Oh

that, I have a great idea. I know as a female you always are looking for romantic ways to show your love."

Stella chose not to point out that, in truth, she was hoping he'd find romantic ways to demonstrate his love. Even her roommate Cece's stoner boyfriend planned a romantic treasure hunt with the treasure being him stretched out nude beside a picnic basket in a wooded glen. She wasn't hoping for a naked picnic, but anything to demonstrate her specialness would be nice.

"Ohhh," she stretched out the word not knowing how to reply. A couple of girls passed by and gave Cam a thorough once over while giggling. Her presence didn't seem to deter them one bit. It reminded her of how lucky she was to have him as a boyfriend when so many other females wanted him.

A bird high up in the tree began to sing. It sounded so carefree and joyous that she envied it. The tiny, feathered creature had a simple life and didn't have to try to understand its mate's cryptic suggestions. It could be singing because the sun was shining or because it just felt like it.

Cam tucked a lock of her hair behind her ear as the wind pulled at her long hair, whipping it around her face. He'd used the same gesture on their initial date. At the time, she considered it incredibly tender. Then, her hair blowing in her eyes somehow shielded her from the effect of his seductive glance. Strange, she needed some sort of a barrier between her and the man she should love. Would she recognize love if it ever happened? Her parents certainly didn't demonstrate it, especially during the last couple of years before the divorce. Even before things got bad, they seemed more like amicable roommates than people in love.

No wonder Cam's persistent pursuit eventually won over her. The fact that one of the hottest guys on campus picked her may have influenced her, although she'd like to think she wasn't that shallow. Cam's preference made her feel important. Her gaze lifted to over his shoulder, avoiding "the look" as the other girls classified it. Only last week, Elena, a fellow student, joked that when Cam turned "the look" on a girl, she'd rip her clothes off without him lifting a finger. Apparently, she hadn't heard about Stella dating the notorious owner of such a compelling glance.

No telling what Stella said or if she even replied when she heard it. Maybe she'd just stumbled away in a stupor. The offhanded remark alerted her that their relationship was unknown. Part of her assumed all his sleeping around was in the past. All she wanted was to keep things the way they were, even if she did have doubts.

Then there was the old Stella. The girl she'd been before her parents' marriage very public implosion. Before that, her worst issue involved her mother snooping in her room and confronting her on Wiccan reading material. Old Stella had no trouble asserting herself. That woman was much more opinionated. Oh, she'd drop the man like he was an STD. *Ooh, she could have done without the metaphor.* Too bad, she couldn't be the old Stella anymore. She wanted to, but just didn't know how to get back there.

Cam smoothed his hand over her long straight fall of blonde hair while using his deepest voice, making her feel like a skittish dog. "Aren't you going to ask what you can do to prove your love?"

The waggle of his eyebrows made the request seem playful, but it wasn't. Oh yeah, she knew the routine. Made it sound like a question, but it served more as an edict. The words felt similar to an anvil dropped on her foot.

Her teeth clamped down on her bottom lip almost willing her not to ask, but she had to. "I'm sure you have a suggestion."

His eyes had lighted up before he planted a quick kiss on her hair. A light touch to her elbow got her moving in the direction of the library building. "Stella, you're working at the computer center still?"

"Yes." Of course, she was. Since it was her only source of money, why wouldn't she? She didn't have the luxury of having rich parents as Cam did. Her steps slowed since she didn't see the use of heading for a building she had no plans to visit today.

"Good. That's what I hoped, but we don't talk much."

He got that right. They ate together, went places, watch television shows he liked and had sex about as often as they could, but talking was the one thing they didn't do. To be more exact, Cam didn't contribute much. Sometimes she might be over at his place folding laundry or fixing dinner while chattering about something she'd learned that day. After a few more attempts at sharing, she realized he didn't pay attention. Shouldn't be too surprising. Most people didn't enjoy learning the way she did.

"Yeah." She knew she wasn't contributing much, rather like asking a blind man for directions. On second thought, a blind man would be more help. Didn't they have to count their steps and everything?

Two smiling co-eds, with shampoo commercial worthy hair and shirts that dipped low to display their twin assets, waved. They spoke in breathy unison, reminding her of the ads for the gentleman clubs. "Hi, Cam."

While he didn't reply, he gave a slow salute that acknowledged their greeting. Seriously? She elbowed him, earning a grunt for her effort. Most girls would wear a camisole or tank top under those shirts. Talk about desperate. *Who were they? Did he sleep with them too? Were they hoping for a return visit?* The thoughts flew through her head, making her uncomfortable. Asking would reveal her insecurities. Instead, she consoled herself with the thought that they were too obvious and fake to attract him. So far, however, her small interaction with the male species demonstrated they often preferred obvious and fake.

They walked in silence for a few steps, allowing the overly friendly girls to pass out of hearing range. "How does me working at the computer center have anything to do with proving my love?"

Instead of answering her question, he bestowed one of his sexy as hell smiles on her. The man must practice in the mirror to do it so effortlessly.

"You're able to get into the personnel files and stuff?" His right brow arched with his inquiry.

"Yeah, but I don't think you want the address of the hot new psych prof that all the girls have been hounding me for." The prof was a cutie, but she didn't dare give out that kind of information on anyone. No doubt, it'd come back to her even if the females in question didn't blab. An inappropriate information release could change her work-study position from the computer lab to landscaping. She'd landed a primo job. The director gave her more responsibility than students who had been there longer because he trusted her, which meant more to her than the badly needed raise.

Cam's brow knitted as his eyes flicked upward. "You mean that short dude who always wears a fedora?"

"Yes."

Cam probably compared him to his own height and found the man lacking. Whatever the instructor lacked in height, he made up for in charisma and wit. At first, she felt rather special knowing she could look up the prof's phone number at any time, not that she'd do anything with it.

"What does he have that'd interest women?" The smug tone of voice indicated the man wasn't any competition in Cam's mind.

Good question and an even harder one to explain to your boyfriend. She settled for a word. "Panache, he has panache."

A snort was his initial reply. "Panache. If you have to go looking for a foreign word that I don't know the meaning of, then it means nothing. It must be some fluke brought on by the climate, hormones, or pumping some chemical into the classroom."

It amused her a little that Cam refused to accept there were other attractive men on campus. He didn't own sex appeal. "Panache means having verve, style—"

He interrupted before she had time to finish her statement.

"I didn't ask what it meant."

Cam hated it when someone gave him directions. He preferred to live in a world of ignorance while her world consisted of gathering information. Talk about opposites.

His fingers entangling with hers surprised her. A new romantic side might be emerging. Her gradual unease that had been growing about their relationship died a fast death with mere handholding. Technically, she considered it more a declaration than the 'bro' arm around her shoulder.

The path wound around the library building and down to a small pond. A narrow dock with wooden Adirondack chairs beckoned students to rest between classes. Watching the ducks glide across the water help eased academic stress. The ducks' plump bodies hinted at their scavenger nature. Good chance they never turn down a chip or a cookie. As their direction veered toward the pond, her irritation eased at missing class. For once, the possibility of a grand gesture loomed in front of her.

Back in high school, some people would do everything from putting up billboards to making videos that made their way online to ask out a girl or even express their interest in a girl. Stella envied the girls and thought it incredibly romantic. Her best friend, Leah, remarked that it was both manipulative and egocentric. It would be hard for a girl to turn down such a public gesture without seeming a jerk. Any guy who chose to share his feelings in such a public venue loved the attention too.

Leah could have been right. It didn't stop Stella from wanting to be the girl who got the unexpected balloon bouquet in class. Even if it was from a boy, she didn't consider date material. It still signaled her desirability. A few males did pursue her with subtle gestures, including walking her to classes, chatting her up, and showing up at places she frequented. It was hard to remember when it stopped. Could have been her junior year when everything else fell apart.

The ducks quacked a noisy welcome the closer they came to the water. Too bad their enthusiasm resulted from whatever tidbit they could solicit. Quacking equaled a natural plea for attention. *Look at me, over here, not my cousin, but me, here, quack, quack.* Ducks resembled humans in that regard.

A small scattering of young weeping willows hugged the banks. The slender bowed branches were not enough to hide a brass quartet that might begin to play once they came into view. Nor was there a splash of color against the browning grass to indicate a picnic. Could be Cam was the creative type and had penned a poem he wanted to recite privately. A sideways glance at her lover didn't reveal any anxiety or even excitement about the upcoming grand gesture.

A park bench boasting a broken slat and hundreds of students' messages either scratched or written squatted by the path. A swoop of his free hand indicated they should stop at the bench. *Seriously, the pond was close, and it would sound so much more romantic in the retelling.*

Cam dropped her hand and sat on the part of the bench that didn't have the broken seat. Great, now she'd have to balance on the edge of the seat or fall off. It wasn't a desirable setting. Ten minutes ago, she didn't even know a romantic gesture was a possibility. Moving her feet about a foot part, she managed to balance herself on a two-inch wood slat. If she lost her balance, she'd fall off the bench or slip back into the hole created by the broken slap. It would probably snag her new jeans too.

Her hands smoothed down the thighs of her jeans. Stella couldn't afford to ruin the jeans since it had taken forever to save up for them. It had been an extravagance, but she felt the jeans were worth it. The polite thing would have been to let her sit on the unbroken part of the bench. Of course, not sitting on the bench at all would have been better. *Concentrate on the moment. Don't ruin it by picking it apart.*

What details could she remember when she pulled it out to reexamine it as an older woman retelling the story for her grandchildren or anyone else who might listen? The sky was blue, which wasn't that unusual. The sun was shining until a fast moving cloud blotted it out making everything a little dimmer.

"Stella, I need you to do me a favor."

Cam's baritone melted her stiff, upright posture, but the words were wrong. Was she wrong about the grand gesture? Could be she wanted it so badly that she'd created indicators that weren't there. An audible sigh escaped her lips. Favors were never good. Usually, they consisted of copying her homework. Some favors were harder such as her mother's request to have nothing to do with her father after the divorce became final. She'd only agreed because she was living with her mother. Ironically, she didn't have to break it because her father had no interest in seeing her. He didn't even bother to show up at her graduation.

"Um, what is it?" She did not intend to promise until she heard it. The acrid smell of duck poop irritated her nose. A rather fitting detail for a romantic gesture gone south.

His hand reached for hers resting on her thigh. Maybe the romantic gesture wasn't totally gone. He might ask her to love him forever or something else like that. If so, she didn't want that type of long-term commitment. After all, Cam was her only real relationship and their connection status was a bit vague.

He held onto her hand but angled his body to look into her eyes. "What's wrong with you? Why are you sitting so weird?"

Working around a broken slat became her problem. She angled her head to look at the broken bench as explanation enough.

"Oh, the bench."

That was it. No offer to switch seats happened. Why had she expected more? Cam liked to refer to himself as a practical man. It sounded better than the ways the frat guys described each other.

"Go on, what's the favor?" Already she regretted asking. Once he told her then, she'd be obligated to do it if she could. Isn't that what friends did for each other? It went double if the people were dating.

"Remember I asked you if you could get into staff files. Have you ever got into the grade books?" He lowered his voice on the last word. It could have been his attempt at discretion. Since the nearest living creatures were ducks, no real issue.

"Well," she hesitated, already disliking the conversation. "Most of that stuff is automated. You take a test in the testing center, and the grade goes into the teacher's grade book. Even the teacher doesn't touch it."

Actually, the teacher could change a grade if they wanted, but no need to tell him that. She'd entered grades before for an older prof who found the computer grade book overwhelming.

"Hmm, I was afraid of that." He released her hand to cradle his head between his hands and sighed loudly.

Part of her wondered if this wasn't bad acting, but she asked anyhow. "What's wrong?"

"Oh, nothing." An audible sniff, then a choking gasp signaling a possible onset of crying.

Couldn't be. He didn't even get choked up when the shelter dog commercials came on. Nothing was a typical male answer. "C'mon, tell me. What's wrong?"

A few more blubbery noises filtered out through his fingers. "I'll lose my scholarship if I can't get my art history grade up."

"Is that all? All you need to do is study. Ask for extra credit." It seemed like an easy enough solution. Her mind caught on the word scholarship. He'd never mentioned being on one before. Instead, he just bragged about how rich his family was.

"Yeah, that might be easy for you, but studying isn't my thing." He sat up long enough to give her the soulful puppy dog eyes. Her heart hurt the same way when she watched a shelter dog commercial, knowing she couldn't adopt the dog.

"I'm not sure what you want me to do. Your family is wealthy. Even if you lose the scholarship, it's no big deal." Not like, it would be with her. She barely scraped by with her scholarship and work-study job. Her mother was always quick to remind her that no money was coming since her father blew it on the cheap skank he chose over his family.

Cam's lips became a little trembly, and then he looked away. "I lied about my family being wealthy."

She wanted to ask why, but he kept talking. It was hard to hear him since he was facing away and the wind increased at that moment.

"Were rich…lost it…that's why the scholarship's important? I need you to change my grade."

She had no trouble hearing that last part. None at all. How horrible. Cam had pride and tried to hide it from her. He probably kept it from her as long as he could. Her hands passed over each other as she wringed them and a sigh escaped her lips.

"I can't do that. Each worker has an ID. Any changes come back to that person. Changing your grade would cost me my scholarship and my job." Knowing her refusal would upset him, she added, "It might even be illegal."

It might not be exactly illegal, but it would cost her dearly. No reason to put it to the test, especially for a male who couldn't come up with one grand gesture or work to solve his own problems. Her heart skipped a beat. The unreliable organ was probably anticipating the fallout from turning down Cam, not that she ever had before if you discounted the times she turned him down for a date before they first went out.

Cam gazed at the pond. The ducks took his action as an invitation and started waddling toward him. The birds initially ignored them when they realized they weren't eating. Could be they expected him to pull something out of his pocket. His lips moved, but whatever he said was too soft to hear.

"Pardon, me. I didn't hear you." She hated asking, afraid her words might anger him. She wrapped her fingers under the bench hunching her shoulders forward expecting not a physical blow, but a verbal one.

Cam continued to stare off into the distance. "I asked who worked with you in the computer lab."

A peculiar question, but one she could answer, considering he inquired in a normal tone of voice. "You know. I've told you before, Noah, Mitch, Lauren, Prashant, Del, and Simon." It wasn't as if she hadn't talked about them before. Apparently, he hadn't been paying attention.

He looked back at her and grinned. "Of course, I remember. Isn't Mitch that geeky guy who has a crush on you?" His laughter punctuated the comment.

Before she had a chance to deny it, he elaborated. "Too nerdy to get laid. It must kill him to see you with me."

Her eyes rolled upward. Why did everything have to come down to sex? Mitch might exemplify geek fashion with his bad haircut and glasses. Still, he was a decent person. "Please, don't talk about him like that. He's sweet. He's even going to copy his notes for me."

This tidbit made Cam laugh even harder. Finally, he slapped his leg and leaned back against the bench. "He's got it bad. Doing little errands for you in hopes of endearing himself to you. Guys like him think that's the way to get lucky."

No way was she interested in Mitch. "He's just a nice guy who likes to help out people." Cam needed to talk about something else. It made her feel disloyal talking about the guy who was taking notes for her. Besides, she ran little errands sometimes—for Cam—and she usually did them to make sure he needed her. Her eyes widened with the realization of how much her behavior resembled Mitch's in always doing things to help. Maybe he did like her.

"Yeah? How many other guys you work with knock themselves out for you?" His smug expression declared he already knew the answer.

Only Mitch. Del and Noah practically spit on her since she jumped over them in seniority. Technically, it was their fault since they often arrived late and left the staff office looking like a war zone. They spent most of their time gaming since the LAN network was incredibly fast and agreed to work third shift to avoid the supervisor. The man found out anyhow, and the assumption was she'd ratted them out after Noah invited her to a game session. Fewer hours and no longer working together served as their only consequence.

She shook her head at the idea of them being nice to her. If she suddenly morphed into an anime character, they might have some interest in her.

Cam's eyes rolled up skyward where several fluffy clouds drifted slowly by unaware of the drama below them. "What about Simon, that foreign guy, and Lauren? Lauren is that a guy or a girl?"

A duck waddled up to her feet and announced his arrival with a few earnest quacks. Frequently, it probably earned him a few chips, bread or pizza crust, or a French fry. Stella opened her purse to search for something to feed the opportunistic bird. Using her teeth, she tore open the cellophane of a package of crushed crackers, while wondering about Cam's sudden outburst of chattiness. This may have been as much as they talked since their first encounter. Why would Cam suddenly be interested in who she worked with and why? *Something felt wrong.*

Scattering the crumbs on the ground, she smiled as the duck thanked his appreciation, scooping up the bits before the other birds reached his bounty.

Instead of answering Cam, she looked toward the lake where the ducks were joining in a type of parade heading their way. In a few seconds, hungry ducks would surround them. Pointing to the feathered mass, she stood. "We need to go."

Cam jumped to his feet immediately and turned to walk up the path they'd come down. Stella had to make a few long-legged strides to catch up. Once they passed under the covered walkway, the birds stopped following. It was almost like there was some invisible fence blocking the creatures from the halls of learning.

Guilt stabbed at her when she thought of the birds hurrying after her sure they'd get something to eat. On the upside, they could use the exercise. The bell tower clock banged out the hour, hurrying students to their destination. *Hard to believe, it was that late already. All that time wasted on hiking across the campus and nothing to show for it.* "Cam, I have to get to my work study job."

Resting her hand on the messenger bag, she turned to speed walk to the technical science building. Cam's voice stopped her.

"Wait."

Could this be it? Finally, the grand gesture?

It only took Cam two steps to reach her side. He flashed his trademark smile and touched her elbow. "Hey, you never answered my question?"

Dear Sweet Goddess. She was tempted to say what question, but she was tired of the entire conversation, and her tone showed it too. "No, Simon is not hot for me. I never see him. Prashant doesn't say much, and when he does, it's something about everything coming out all right in the end. Lauren is a shy girl with thick glasses and an inferiority complex who barely says two words to anyone. Anything else?"

Cam held up his hands. "Whoa. Sounds like someone needs to go take a chill pill." He turned and jogged away without a goodbye or even a wave. Stella watched as a trio of girls stopped and watched him pass. Yeah, he did look good running, and he knew it.

The charm of dating one of the hottest males on campus had its downside. All the other girls lusting after him sucked. On the upside that made him more of a prize, but any time with Cam served as an emotional workout. The man picked up her insecurities, her need for affection, and confidence and, threw all of them high in the air as in juggling balls. Often her confidence would wing upward when she was with him, but when she wasn't, her insecurities came crashing down making her wonder if his interest had already moved elsewhere. Unfortunately, she could already feel his attention waning. Without him, she'd be alone on the campus as before. Sure, she kept busy with her homework and work-study job, but then there were those long weekend hours when no one came to visit.

CHAPTER TWO

S TELLA ADJUSTED THE paper to better analyze Professor Emeril's loopy handwriting. Out of the work-study students, she was the only one able to decipher his notes. Sometimes she wondered if he could even read them. Her knowledge of world history was good enough to enable her to fill in the illegible parts. In a math major's mind, Eurasia might become Europe, which was far from being the same thing.

As if he heard his name, Mitch pushed open the computer lab door. "Hey, you."

Stella looked up with a smile. "Hey, you, yourself. How was class? Did I miss anything mind boggling?"

Mitch pushed up his sliding glasses with one finger and shrugged his shoulders. "Not really. Same old. Same old."

A sheath of stapled notes fluttered to her desk. She picked up the thick pack. "Wow, pretty impressive notes. Thanks."

"Not really, I only wrote on one side." His backpack hit the floor as he sat down and flicked on his monitor.

Stella picked up the folder that had his work assignment in it. Other students thought the computer lab assistants just sat around and waited for someone to use the computers, but there was more involved than that. Noah and Del accused her of informing their supervisor about their gaming without realizing the obvious reason for their discovery was they never got their work done. It surprised her that they still had jobs.

"You only have notes to type into the SharePoint database."

He took the folder and groaned. "Not my fav."

His remark was typical Mitch. How well she knew him was surprising. Her eyes drifted over him. Cam declaring Mitch had a crush on her was probably a joke. Still, she considered the male hunched over the computer. Could it be true?

Mitch, unlike Cam, spent most of his time trying to *not* garner attention. He was as tall as Cam, maybe taller, but no one would know the way he hunched his shoulders and slumped in his seat trying to be invisible. She'd asked her roommate if she knew him after Mitch had mentioned Cece was in two of his classes. Despite Stella's detailed description of Mitch, her roommate denied knowing him.

If he had a crush on her, how should she handle it? Her fingers rested on the keyboard, her thoughts in disarray. Taking a deep breath, she focused on the messy notes she was transcribing. There was plenty of regular work for her once she finished the notes. Her boss didn't mind her helping the faculty out with light typing. Her reward consisted of a warm smile and a plain envelope. Inside the envelope rested a few crisp bills. Their denomination depended on how difficult the work was and how generous the professor felt. Mitch had cautioned her to set a standard rate to prevent the staff from taking advantage of her.

She didn't need things to be awkward between her and

Mitch because they worked together. The slight patter of Mitch's fingers racing across the keyboard caused a stab of envy. No one on campus could type as fast or as accurately as he did. Too bad that wasn't a characteristic that girls wanted like rock hard abs.

The computer lab door swung open from Lauren's push. The reticent female didn't typically work with Stella, except when there was some test to proctor. A glance at the calendar listed a philosophy exam. "Hi."

A plexiglass wall separated Lauren from the student testing center. The girl nodded at her as she passed on the way to her desk on the other side of the administration section. Not known for her sparkling conversation, it was a challenge for Lauren to monitor the students. Most often, she only checked off as they signed in on the various computers.

The handsome, but not prepared, males sometimes tried to solicit more time or even actual answers. Somehow, they believed they had the right to such rewards that their plainer counterparts, who actually studied for the test, didn't have. In another testing center on another campus, maybe they would have received the benefit but not here. The outright flirting rattled Lauren so much that often Stella had to intercede.

At times, a buffed male would be lounging in a chair, sometimes with his hands propped behind his head, expecting Lauren to trot back with the needed answers. Instead, Stella would tap on the glass to get his attention, while mouthing the word, "No," or most often, "Try studying."

Mitch usually enjoyed the encounters. Even getting up to be able to see the shocked expression on the male's face.

Occasionally, she had to go to the actual room because there were other students studying and knocking on the window would disturb them. The male in question maintained his smug expression until she whispered the same words she'd have mouthed. It made her wonder if Cam ever pulled the same stunt. If so, what were his results?

Her fingers hit the keys a little harder than necessary. Wasn't his inquiry about her changing his grade the same scenario? The only difference was she was sleeping with him, and he figured it was a done deal. Most men would assume as much.

"Angry typing, much?" Mitch called out to her, wiggling his eyebrows disrupting her tension.

The way she was going, she'd end up breaking the keyboard. "Oh, yeah. Never mind. Thanks for pointing it out."

Her fingers slowed, softening the impact of each finger on the key. The students trickled in to take the test. The murmur of voices alerted her that obviously a few were not following protocol. A large sign listing the rules had no talking as the first. Lauren was too timid to say anything. Normally, it wasn't an issue since the students didn't come in huge groups.

The talking continued loudly enough to carry through the Plexiglas. Getting up she weaved through the long tables crowded with monitors and CPUs only to find Lauren staring at the offenders with the same look of horror most people used for approaching death.

Since the voices were feminine, she knew it wasn't Lauren's usual kryptonite, the hot guy. Two female students with perfect hair and enough eye makeup to keep the cosmetic industry in business chattered loudly, ignoring the other students around them who were casting reproachful looks their way. Ah yes, she knew the type. The world revolved around them and they didn't give a damn about anyone else. Probably even argued with the prof about tests being out of style and an unfair measure of their ability.

No way could Lauren deal with them. They'd look through her and pretend they didn't even see her. Thankfully, Stella had her own experience with mean girls from high school. Both she and Leah medaled in mean girl avoidance and sly innuendoes that flew past the vicious females.

Opening the connecting door a little louder than she should, she stood in the doorway. Everyone looked up, even the chattering girls. Leah's Nana once informed her how to handle difficult people. *Make an entrance, assume an attitude, show no fear, and make a statement, then leave.*

Her hand landed on the panicked Lauren's shoulder, as she said, "I'll deal with it." This earned her a weak smile.

Shoulders back, Stella flicked her long blonde hair over her shoulders. She nodded to the other testing students and approached the problem women with a confident air. "It has come to my attention that you failed to heed testing protocol."

The first girl pulled out a compact, checking her makeup. Her friend stared up Stella with a quizzical expression. Pointing to the sign, Stella enunciated the words slowly and loudly enough for the other students to hear. "No talking in the lab."

The girls looked at each other in surprise. One of the girls angled her head in Stella's direction, the calculation on her face obvious, and said, "You can't tell us what to do."

Oh, she wanted to play it that way. Stella expected as much. A slight motion of her hand signaled Lauren to cut the power to their units. Their screens went blank. The girls were too intent on Stella's reaction to notice their monitors, but the other students saw it.

One student voiced his observation. "Hey look, their computers were shut down."

Another student snickered. Bossy girl's face reddened as her mouth dropped open. Her head swiveled back to her friend, asking for help.

Stella placed her hands on her hips remembering from psychology that posture made her appear more intimidating. "You're done here. Come back when you can follow the rules. Better yet, maybe a blue book exam would suit you better."

One of the girls immediately stood up, teetering a little in her sky-high heels. Shouldering her expensive purse, she remarked over her shoulder. "We'll be back when the cute guys are working."

Her friend got up more slowly, returning Stella's glare with a malice-filled one of her own. "Don't think it's over, bitch. You may be head witch, here, but not for long."

Instead of answering, she merely watched the girls leave. Silence at the right time could be powerful too. Too many people made the mistake of thinking they had to respond to everything. Miss I'm All That thought she'd wounded her by calling her a witch. *Hah, she had no clue how right she was. As for being a bitch, well it took one to know one.*

A few of the students started clapping. A couple more

thanked her. She nodded, accepting their appreciation and muttered, "No problem."

Keeping her back straight, she strode toward the open door, sanctuary. She preferred to be on the anonymous side of the Plexiglas. Closing the door behind her, she released a huge sigh. *Thank the Goddess that was over.*

Lauren popped to her feet and wrapped her in a huge hug. "Thank you so much, I could never have gotten them to leave."

Stella was about to admit her doubts about getting the two to leave when Mitch came over. Lauren still held her in an impromptu embrace when Mitch awkwardly patted her on the back.

The slight contact left behind a psychic handprint. Her eyes met his over Lauren's shoulder. Did Mitch follow the Goddess? Have a bit of magick in him? Technically, everyone possessed some earth magick, but few knew how to wield it. Often simple divination magic came under headings like hunches and lucky guesses. Others blessed with the ability to enchant often used their skills as a form of manipulation. Most who identified with the earth-based religions enjoyed spending time in nature.

His warm hazel eyes twinkled as he spoke, "You were glorious."

Glorious? No one had ever called her glorious. A bubble of warmth expanded in her chest. If all it took to be glorious was to kick two mean girls out of the lab, she might do it more often. The problem was if she did, she'd end up losing her job because one of their daddies would accuse her of harassment, terroristic threatening, or similar nonsense.

A huge smile blossomed on Mitch's face, animating his features. Goodness, he was even handsome when he forgot about trying to make himself invisible. A decent haircut, new frames, and more self-confidence and he'd be the one the mean girls came back to attempt to wrap around their manicured fingers. The thought dimmed the warmth spreading through her. None of them was worthy of Mitch.

A familiar scent rode the air. It didn't blend with the smell of dust, monitor wipes, or the metal smell of CPUs. Her nostrils flared a tiny bit as she tried to draw the aroma in. Sandalwood, she was almost sure of it. Sandalwood incense was a favorite for meditation, but there would be no incense in the lab. It could be sandalwood oil, which sometimes showed up in men's cologne and love potions.

Lauren's tight embrace finally relaxed as she dropped her arms. Stella shrugged her shoulders. "All in a day's work, I guess." Saluting the two of them, she clicked her heels together and walked back to her desk.

Their laughter followed her. Lauren's sounded nervous and forced while Mitch's was mellow. Just hearing his laughter made her feel good. The idea of him having a crush on her wasn't as preposterous as it once seemed. Her fingers went up to fuss with her hair, smoothing over the long length to see if any strands were out of place.

The only male in the work area was Mitch, and he could be wearing cologne. The distance between their computers measured a meter, which made it easy to pass folders without having to get up. In a matter of seconds, Mitch returned to typing fast, his head moving slightly between the paper and his computer screen.

Stella memorized chunks of info and then typed while occasionally glancing at the keys for reassurance that her fingers were where they should be, especially after she misspelled a word.

Work awaited her if she wanted to earn any extra money. As it was, everything she earned disappeared into the giant gaping mouth of the college. Nothing was cheap on campus, from snacks to copies. The on-campus stores took advantage of the students by hiking up the prices. Those with cars made runs to discount stores. Still others depended on a weekly check from their parents. Her mouth twisted to one side at the thought of parents. Hers had forgotten her. Dear old dad appeared to be in a hurry to recreate a new family with his young wife. Hard to believe when he emphatically told her having her ruined his life. Without her existence, he'd had left her mother years ago.

The baby tidbit came via Leah, who still lived in their hometown. Leah saw Stella's father more than she did. He'd recognized Leah and made a point of saying, "hello." He had to know her friend would convey the info to her. Maybe that's what he wanted. *Look, Stella, I'm happy now with my new wife and son.* A muttered curse slipped out.

Mitch stopped typing and regarded her with a furrowed brow. 'Hey, are you okay?"

Embarrassed that she'd drawn his attention, she grabbed for a convenient excuse. "I broke a nail."

Her eyes flicked down to her ragged, short nails that she'd

regularly gnawed to the quick.

Mitch didn't call her on it. He lifted an eyebrow and returned to typing. He knew she'd lied, but he was too polite to pry.

A dozen keystrokes later, her maudlin thoughts caught up with her. Her mother never sent her money to tide her over. Even Cece's parents sent her an occasional care package filled with snacks, toiletries, office supplies, and a check. The best she got was an occasional pamphlet about the torments of hell if she should die today without repenting of her evil ways. No one could ever accuse her mother of being overly affectionate or loving. The occasions when she'd displayed a little bit of pride when Stella won a merit award disappeared about the time the divorce happened. Her mother's crutch during the entire ordeal was a small church she started attending. After the divorce, Stella stayed away from the house as much as possible due to the ghosts that hung out there. Not spirits that were unwilling to move on, but rather memories of happier times. If she stayed at home more, she could have provided emotional support for her mother, instead of leaving her vulnerable to the dubious care of The Last Days and Holy Resurrection Tabernacle pastor.

Stella had never stepped inside the shabby white building despite her mother's repeated attempts to get her to attend. At first, she might have gone, to keep peace in the house, but the judgmental messages placed on the marquee outside kept her feet planted firmly on the other side of the doors. Everything from *Repent Now or Burn Forever* and *Enjoy your sin today, pay for it eternally.*

The smell of sandalwood grew stronger as Mitch's shadow fell over her. He bent slightly to rest one hand near her keyboard. "Hey, what's going on with you?"

Her behavior must be odd if Mitch noticed. She meant to use a cramps excuse, which weirded out boys and stopped future questions. A slight turn of her head caused her to look directly into his sympathetic eyes. "Truth is I was thinking about my mother and how she hooked up with this fire and brimstone church. About the only communication, we ever have now is my monthly reminder that I'm damned to hell."

She wanted to call back her revealing words. Maybe Mitch belonged to a similar church. Instead of acting horrified, he reached for his chair and drew it to face hers before he sat.

His index finger pushed up his slipping glasses as he sat. "I understand. My older sister went through a stage like that when her husband left her. I think she thought if she prayed hard enough he'd come back. He didn't. I always wondered why she wanted someone who didn't want her."

His insightful words allowed her to release the breath she'd been holding. "Maybe that's what happened to my mother. She hadn't been too religious until Dad left. We used to only show up at Our Lady of Sorrows for the major holidays, Christmas and Easter."

Mitch nodded, making her feel he heard her. When was the last time anyone had truly listened to her? She tried to remember. Talking with most people was a bit like a computer search. They responded to keywords that had something to do with them. Going away to school kept her distant from her mother's machinations, but it also limited any interaction she had with her best friend, Leah. Lately, she'd been the one cutting conversations short with Leah to be with Cam.

Mitch touched her hand. "Go on. What about your father? Is he still alive?"

Still alive that was a peculiar comment. "Yes, he is, very much to my mother's regret." *Did she want him dead too? It would be easier to forgive a dead father than one who chose to write her off.*

Her top teeth worried her bottom lip. Did she sound too much like one of the callers on a radio therapy show? Would Mitch feel awkward working with her in the future?

His hand went up to his glasses, probably to push the slipping glasses up, but he pulled them off instead and placed them near her keyboard. Stella blinked at the transformation the simple action made. *Talk about a Superman move.* Her eyes dropped to his chest wondering if he'd rip open his checked shirt to reveal a colorful spandex suit decorated with a giant S underneath it.

Using a bent finger, he rubbed the area between his eyebrows. "Be glad you have a father. Right now, things might not seem too great, but at least there's a future where the two of you can develop a better relationship."

His hand half hid his face, which may have been his intention, but it didn't disguise the pain in his words.

"What happened to your father?"

"Heart attack. He died when I was thirteen. We'd argued about me cutting the grass. I was going to do it. I just wanted to finish the level on my video game first."

"How horrible!" Stella placed her hand on Mitch's just as

Lauren passed behind the two of them. *Let her think what she wants.* "I hope you don't blame yourself."

Mitch shrugged his shoulders and looked up briefly at Stella. His glassy eyes revealed his guilt-laden state. "My mother told me it wasn't my fault. His family had a history of heart disease. That along with too much fast food and no exercise caused it."

Stella almost felt like she was witnessing a drowning and didn't know what to do. "It would have happened no matter what. You're not to blame." Her hand squeezed his, realizing her problems seemed mundane in retrospect.

"Yeah, you're right. I guess. I just hate that our last words were in anger. Like most teenagers, I disappointed my father. I always wanted to do what I wanted to do and never what interested him. As a kid, we camped and fished together. As I got older, I was more into video games, especially the role-playing games. If I'd continued to canoe and hike with my father, he'd have been in better shape."

Whoa, he might be right, but she couldn't tell him that. "Mitch, listen to me." Her free hand touched his face to gain his attention. "You were a child while your father was an adult. As the adult, he made the decision to be physically fit or not. He could have exercised with your mother, a friend, or even by himself. There is no reason to blame yourself. In the end, Fate has her way."

Mitch's lips tipped up in a weak smile. "You suck at giving pep talks."

His words surprised a half-laugh that ended in a cough. Clearing her throat, she managed to reply, "Yeah, that's what

I've been told." The warmth of his hand reminded her that they were still holding hands. His larger hand engulfed hers making her feel safe if only for a moment. It was a false security.

Security, safety, believing your world would keep spinning in its usual fashion were all things that she'd taken for granted not too long ago. Tons of parents divorced. Probably, over half the students at the university or maybe even more, which meant she had no excuse for feeling sorry for herself. *Suck it up, Stella.* Why couldn't her inner drill sergeant comprehend her feeling of rootlessness? In some ways, she was a jellyfish.

The current carried the jellyfish. A wave would sometimes hurl the gelatinous creature into an unwary swimmer. Without an actual brain, the jellyfish only reacted by wrapping its long arms around a leg. It might be holding on for dear life or assuming whatever it touched was dinner. In the end, it left a stinging sensation behind, a reminder of its brief contact. *Goddess, she hoped she wasn't like that. Hurting everyone, she touched.* Might do her good to watch her interactions if she could be so toxic.

Perhaps, feeling the same awkwardness after their shared emotional episode, Mitch released her hand while pushing back with his feet to propel the rolling chair back to his desk. "Time to get back to work."

She watched him pivot the chair and immediately return to typing as if nothing had happened. A thought nudged at her consciousness leaving behind the image of her scarring everyone she bumped against. "Mitch, did you ever play any video games after your father's heart attack?"

He continued typing, didn't even look up. Stella thought he hadn't heard her until he stopped typing and stared at the keyboard. Finally, he murmured, "Not a one." He remained silent for a few more seconds, then, he looked up. "Could you hand me my glasses."

CHAPTER THREE

ALL THAT TIME, he was only pretending to type. Grief could resemble a boa constrictor wrapping itself around the victim and squeezing out all hope. She certainly didn't have any sage wisdom to offer. Instead, she picked up his glasses and polished them on the edge of her shirt, before handing them over.

Flipping the page of her notes, she positioned her hands to start typing, but a prickling at the back of her neck distracted her. It reminded her of the time the bald man in a trench coat followed her around town when she was only ten. Her mother, busy shopping, handed her some money to go to a nearby ice cream shop only a few blocks away, and she knew how to cross the street safely. It should have been an uneventful trip until she noticed the man's reflection in a window.

Her first thought was it was a hot day, and he didn't need a coat. The ice cream shop was within sight when she decided he was following her. Breaking into a run, she'd dashed into the store. The man stood outside and glared at her through the glass emblazoned with the shop's name. Terror squeezed her heart for a moment as their eyes met. His cold eyes glittered, confirming she'd slipped through his fingers. She never told her mother about the man, somehow thinking she'd done something wrong to cause him to pursue her. Good chance her mother would have blamed it on reading too many mystery books. She remembered what it felt like, rather similar to the spot on the back of her neck now. Covering her neck with one hand, she swiveled her chair only to meet Lauren's baleful stare.

What was wrong? Stella's eyes drifted to the testing center. Most of the students had left. No problem, there, what could be her issue? She'd never had any difficulties with Lauren before, but her current glare declared she'd willingly plunge a knife into Stella's back. *Foolish, paranoia, she was getting as bad as her mother was. Think happy thoughts.* Currently, she didn't have a backlog of cheerful thoughts, but maybe she could do something that would make Cam happy and get his mind off her accessing academic files. Good Goddess, she couldn't change his grades. There had to be another way to show her love.

Cam had explicitly mentioned his upcoming birthday. A casual comment about how much he enjoyed gazing at the night sky stuck in her mind. It would also be something they could do together. Her intention was to get him a telescope she'd seen at the nearby pawnshop. With her luck, an astronomy buff could wander into the seedy little store, recognize the value of the Orion refractor telescope and snatch it up before she could.

Cam definitely expected something. Instead of finding out his birthday by social media or even looking it up in the database, he'd told her. On their second date. If you could call it a date since it occurred at an off campus Laundromat. Most of their dates were rather un-date-like, but then again most of the college populace either hung out or hooked up. The formal ritual of asking a girl out for a date had fallen by the wayside.

Her eyes shifted to Mitch, who stared intently at his monitor. She'd bet he'd be the type to ask a girl out on a real date as opposed to a general invite to a frat party. The man might even iron his clothes, comb the campus newspaper for ideas on what to do, and show up with a single rose. *Yeah, that sounded like Mitch.* Thinking about how adorable he'd look standing in the doorway clutching a flower, her lips twitched.

The man in question looked up. "What's with the goofy smile, and why are you staring at me?"

Caught. What could she say? Why was she staring at him and speculating what he'd be like on a date? Rubbing her open hand over her face, she stalled and wiped away her smile. *Think.*

"I, um, I was thinking of my second date with Cam. We went to the Laundromat." Her excuse sounded lame. Some might consider confiding her dating life to her male co-worker weird. Her roommate Cece had such a snarky side she kept as much as she could from her. Leah knew about Cam, but never acted that thrilled about him, which annoyed Stella. After all, she never made snide comments when Leah started dating Dylan. At least, Mitch would never gossip.

Mitch turned back to the monitor, snorted. "Whoa, why didn't I think of asking a girl out to view my laundry? I now realize my dating techniques are all wrong. Maybe I could follow up the next date with a trip to the grocery."

Stella wanted to protest, but at least three of their *dates* had been the grocery. Mitch's words made it sound stupid and lame. It wasn't like that. "Hey, now. The hum of dryers and the overwhelming smell of fabric sheets really set the scene."

She grimaced realizing she had once considered it romantic. The mother with the three screaming toddlers finally left leaving behind a silence broken up by the swish of a washer and the dual drone of dryers. Late on a Friday night, the place echoed eerily with its emptiness. It was then he mentioned his birthday, hinting broadly for something special. He probably meant sex, but since they were now already sleeping together, the telescope seemed her best bet.

Mitch slapped the desk, startling her. She turned to stare at him as he held up both hands dramatically.

"That's it. Why did no one ever tell me? If I rub my body with dryer sheets, I'll be irresistible to the opposite sex."

Her eyes rolled upward on their own. "You're not taking me seriously. I'm trying to explain what I was thinking. You make jokes about dryer sheets. I was attempting to think of a great gift for Cam's birthday. He mentioned his birthday on our second date at the"

"Laundromat." Mitch finished her statement. "God, he told you his birthday. So you could go get him something, I bet. Something special, too." He added eyebrow waggle for emphasis.

Did every male use the same gesture to denote something risqué? "It wasn't like that." She denied the implications, even if it had been like that. Mitch never liked Cam and didn't try to hide it either. "Besides, what's so wrong about telling someone when your birthday is? It's not that out of the ordinary."

"Yeah, right." He turned back to the screen, giving her his back, which ended their conversation.

His words resurrected doubts. "What do you mean? I know you meant something?"

His silence and scrolling down the screen indicated he'd shut her out, which surprised her. Normally, Mitch wasn't moody. Finally, he muttered. "I bet you don't know when my birthday is?"

"Of course, I do. We've worked together for over two months. There's no reason I wouldn't know your birthday. We're friends." As she spoke, she made a mental inventory of everything she knew about Mitch. The sound of slamming file cabinet drawers indicated Lauren remained in a snit. The noise didn't make it any easier to think either.

She should know this. Her hand slid closer to her mouse. *A quick peek at the personnel records would help her faulty memory.*

"No fair looking it up."

He guessed her intentions. Damn. "Obviously, I'm a crummy friend. I can't remember your birthday. Sue me."

Swiveling his chair, he turned to stare at her. "The reason you don't know my birthday is I never told you. I never said anything because I didn't expect you to do anything for me. A guy who tells you his birthday expects a big deal. The fact that he told you on the second date makes it even more suspicious."

Her hand shot out and wrapped around his arm. "Not so fast, boyo."

He laughed. "What are you now, an Irish gangster from the thirties?"

He was right; she sounded bizarre. "It's your fault." Noting his raised eyebrows, she added, "Mostly." She dropped her hand, bit her bottom lip, and wanted to ask why it looked suspicious, but was afraid of the answer.

He inhaled deeply, and then let it out in a loud sigh. "I'm sorry I said anything, but can't you see Cam is using you."

No, not this argument again. She glanced at his lips pulled into a frown. Hadn't they already had this discussion before? Wait that was Leah. Stella denounced Leah's concerns calling her jealous, which was ridiculous since she'd been with Dylan forever. "Explain how mentioning his birthday is using me?"

"You didn't ask for it. He offered it, even mentioned he'd be open to gifts. Told you on the second *date*." He made a point of emphasizing the word date, implying their date was no more than laundry duty.

Everything was true. As a tech geek, Mitch knew how to manipulate data. Cam was everything a girl could want if you liked six pack abs, great hair, and a gorgeous smile. Stella almost missed Mitch's comment as she mentally searched for other attributes Cam might have.

"Wonder how many other girls he's mentioned his birthday to."

Her first response was to deny he hadn't told anyone, but how did she know? He could have made up flyers and handed them out to the various sororities. Mitch's logic was taking her down a path she didn't want to go.

He muttered, "Forget about it." When she fell silent.

Goddess, she wasn't sure, how they even got into this discussion but wished they hadn't. A lack of drawer slamming caused her to glance in Lauren's direction who still shot daggers at her. Strange.

She resumed typing as Mitch stood and walked out of the room. Good chance he left to avoid the tension. More likely, he went to grab a soda. Her fingers flew across the keys making up for the time she wasted discussing Laundromat rendezvous and the importance of telling birthday dates. Green and red squiggles appeared under various words indicating that while typing fast, it wasn't always accurate.

Thanks a lot, Mitch. Now I have to go back and proof everything. It wasn't like she didn't already proof usually, but now she'd have more to correct. Her fingers slowed a bit as she tried to read each paragraph carefully, making sure she made sense out of the semi-illegible notes. The tiny clock at the right side of the screen reminded her that she had plenty of regular work left on her shift and no real time for her extra duties.

The pneumatic door springs caused the fire doors that enclosed the lab to close with an ominous clang, rather like the sound of the prison gates closing. She looked up to see Mitch brandishing two chip bags.

"Snack run?"

"Of a sort." Mitch shrugged and placed a bag of multigrain chips on her desk. "Consider it a peace offering."

The brightly colored bag drew her attention, especially since it was her favorite. Hunger whetted her appetite even more. Her fingers reached for the shiny sack as she considered her actions toward her co-worker. "Thank you. I'm sorry if I went all crazy over the birthday issue. You're right. No one goes around announcing their birthday unless they want a gift or a big party."

She certainly hadn't. Cam hadn't asked hers, and she hadn't offered. There didn't seem to be a point since they might not be dating then anyhow. Ripping open the bag, she picked out the first chip and allowed it to sit on her tongue, appreciating the mix of flavors and the tang of saltiness. She'd denied herself the delicious luxury for quite a while. The second chip she consumed faster and the third chip even more so.

The real reason she never told Cam her birthday was she didn't want to be disappointed again. Last year, her father, too involved with his new family, did nothing for her birthday. Her mother had the nerve to send a note about contributing to the crazy church in her name. More likely, it bought her penance, forgiveness, or something. Leah had sent her a present, but the campus postal service delivered it to the wrong dorm. She didn't get it until almost a week later.

That made her last birthday a particularly depressing day. Wrapping her fingers around the last chips in the bag, she shoved them into her mouth and crunched down hard, causing crumbs to slide down her face. The feeling of hopelessness threatened to return. Another bag of chips landing on her keyboard interrupted her visit to birthdays past.

Mitch gestured to the bag. "Looks like you could use another bag."

Chips packed her cheeks, most likely giving her a chipmunk appearance. She looked away from Mitch, in the direction of a nearby dark monitor that reflected back her image. A wild-eyed woman on the verge of tears with plump cheeks and food crumbs dotting her face stared back. A tissue wiped away the crumbs. Chewing and swallowing slimmed her cheeks, but nothing could remove the lost look from her eyes.

Feeling thirsty, she reached for the water bottle she kept by her monitor. It wasn't there, another casualty of her meeting with Cam. The water bottle she usually brought sat back in her dorm room doing her no good. The fountain at the end of the hall between the restrooms would serve.

The deserted hallway gave her time to think as her footsteps echoed on the cement floor. If this were a movie, something sinister would jump out of one of the darkened doorways. Currently, her thoughts provided enough of a fright factor. Somewhere she'd lost her way, going from a confident female who was going to change the world into a distant individual most people managed to look through. It was no wonder she found Cam's interest so gratifying.

Three long drinks later and a wipe down with a damp paper towel rid her of most of her crumbs. It was time to return. Thank goodness, she worked in a facility most students seldom used, probably unaware that part of their tuition paid for use of the lab.

About the only time, students showed up was to print out papers. The younger profs encouraged online submission. This helped when paper completion happened two minutes short of the midnight deadline. Nope, no one to witness her minor meltdown, except for Mitch and Lauren, and Mitch would be cool about it. Lauren had mood swings, which meant it could go either way depending on the day.

Her back to the room, she held the door handle causing the door to swing close slowly and not announce her return. Fighting against the automatic assist that usually slammed the heavy door shut tested her bicep muscle. When she wasn't sure how much longer she could hold the heavy door, it clicked closed. She pivoted and ran into a solid, masculine body. Her nose buried in his chest, and she inhaled the variety of aromas. The predominant one was a sandalwood and a hint of dryer sheet along with a clean, underlying scent she identified as Mitch.

His hands wrapped around her shoulders steadied her. *Could it get any worse?* "Umm, sorry." She looked up into Mitch's face.

"I was worried about you. If you hadn't come back, then I'd have looked for you to see if you were okay." A blush painted his cheeks. His hands fell from her shoulders as he stepped back, allowing her access to her desk.

Tucking an errant lock of hair behind her ear, she moved around him. While her back was to him, she spoke, "That's sweet of you." Looking at him full on might cause her to choke on the phrase. Stray dogs had nothing on Mitch. He could convey sincerity and promise absolute devotion by softening his eyes. She wondered if anyone noticed other than her.

"Yeah, I'm sweet like that." He took a step toward her as she slid into her chair. "Are you really okay?"

The easy answer would be yes. *What was he actually asking her? Was she okay that her boyfriend was a bit of a user? Mitch had no idea how right he was on that one. Was she alright that her family put the dys in dysfunctional? Was she okay after her manic chip frenzy? That was probably the real question.* "Yeah, I'm okay. Maybe a little junk food deprived. I went a little crazy there."

"Good." His hand settled on her shoulder for a second, then left, as if he'd overstepped his bounds.

Stella wanted to tell him to put his hand back. For a moment, she'd felt a connection, a sense of belonging and understanding. Something she could never achieve with Cam no matter what the body part. Mitch stood behind her rather like a shield protecting her. The silence wasn't awkward, rather the opposite. Finally, he spoke breaking the bond.

"May first."

What was that supposed to mean? The date dropped out of nowhere made no sense.

Mitch continued in a voice too low for Lauren to hear. "It's your birthday."

"Of course, I know it's my birthday." He'd looked it up while she was gone. "Why did you look it up when I went to get a drink?"

He didn't make mention of her chip eating frenzy. Besides getting a drink, she was more on a search for her mental stability that she'd misplaced.

"I did look it up." The stray dog steals your heart look slipped over his face again. "But not today, the day we met."

The memories of that day filtered back. David, the tech lab supervisor, convinced the new staffers that some cosmic disaster equivalent to the apocalypse would happen if they ever used their access inappropriately. He'd certainly frightened her, but Mitch didn't seem to have any fears about peeking into her file. Could be that he realized David was all bluster and ignored the warning. Then again, the problem with tech-savvy students staffing the lab is that they were capable of devising ways to get around security protocol.

"Oh." That was the best she could do. She wanted to ask why, but she knew. Her birthday was important to him because he was interested. Mitch would have possibly devised a whole array of birthday surprises if the two of them ever were a couple.

He shrugged his shoulders and gave her a sheepish smile. "Sorry. I don't want you to think I'm stalking you or anything."

"No problem." She uttered her standard reply, never giving his behavior a sinister slant for a moment. Leah explained after her sister Nora's amazing rescue how her sister sensed her kidnapper's evilness before the incident. There was no evil in Mitch.

The sound of music drifted through the area. A band featuring a long guitar solo with the lead singer shouting a few unidentifiable words about every eight measures. Stella craned her neck trying to identify the source. Rules forbade students bringing their iPods into the testing center because they could insert answer info onto it. If grades were money, and they often were with scholarships, then college served as a training ground for future embezzlers. Every known way to cheat the system occurred at least once, and dozens more ways would pop up before the end of the semester.

Lauren's iPod lay on the counter ear buds unplugged. It

could be a simple oversight, but Lauren sat beside it with the earplugs in her hands, daring Stella to say something. Pushing up out of the chair, she walked toward the testing center. Since no bent head worked feverishly to finish a timed exam, Stella couldn't complain about disturbing the students and refused to mention it bothered her. For some reason, she felt it was Lauren's intention. Why give her the satisfaction?

Sighing deeply, Stella realized now that she was in Lauren's area; she'd have to make some comment on her appearance. "Any more exams?"

Lauren jammed the jack back into the MP3 player, silencing it. "No. That's it."

Stella glanced at the clock on Lauren's monitor. About twenty minutes left on the shift. The brief look at the screen identified a dating advice website. It didn't matter what site she was on since she was only supposed to monitor the exams. 'You could shut down and leave early."

Mistrust peeked out of Lauren's eyes while her lips pinched as if she'd bitten into a lemon. "That would cut me out of twenty minutes." Her gaze flicked back to Mitch. Odd that she'd look at Mitch. Technically, Stella oversaw Lauren, not Mitch.

"Not really, I can turn off your computer." Suspicion still flickered in Lauren's eyes. "Maybe you can ask Mitch to do it."

The idea brought a sly smile to her face. "I'll do that." She opened her messenger bag and dumped assorted snacks, water bottle, and iPod into the bag with one swipe.

In an effort to appear busy, Stella moved around the exam center, moving mouses to see if the screens would flicker to life. Lauren walked over to Mitch's station and bent down to whisper in his ear. Her actions surprised Stella because she didn't think the girl had that much boldness. She'd figured wrong.

On a hunch, she went back to Lauren's computer. An open file materialized with Mitch's name at the top. It included his schedule, his dorm assignment, his home address, his phone number, and his birthday, which was yesterday.

Talk about a major crush. No doubt, Mitch was supposed to find this little token of her obsession, then knowing how she felt would be equally smitten with her. A stupid middle school plan, although it might work. College could be a very lonely time as opposed to the big party most high school seniors envisioned. Instead of alerting Mitch to her find, Stella closed down the page.

Yesterday was his birthday. What did she do? Nothing, when he'd saved her butt on more than one occasion due to a Cam emergency, which was usually only an emergency in Cam's eyes. She should do something.

Strolling back to her station, she wondered how she'd approach him. Hearing her footsteps or more likely it was the lights she turned off as she cleared each area, Mitch turned at her approach. The third shift used a very limited area. Although the lab was supposed to be open twenty-four hours, very few students burned the midnight oil, probably not relishing a walk back in the dark.

"Did you send Lauren over to whisper in my ear?"

Why would she do such a thing? "No, that was all her. I told her she could leave early and she doubted my generosity. I suggested even that you could close down her computer."

"Yeah. I'm not sure what I did to deserve the honor. Oh well, only fifteen more minutes." He made a face. "This utility scan should finish by then."

"If so, you got more done than me. I'll be taking work with me." Seated in her chair, she turned it away from him. Make it look casual. Staring at her monitor, she asked. "What did you do for your birthday yesterday?"

"Ha! I knew you would look it up. You're so predictable." A broad grin displayed the one incisor that lapped over the other.

The predictable label didn't appeal. She had no desire to confess where she'd picked up the information, either. "I asked you what you did. Maybe a cake?"

His smile disappeared as suddenly as it came. "My mom sent me a card with a strange letter in it."

"What was so strange about it?" At least, he had a parent who wrote to him. Her mother's scribbled words on pamphlets detailing her fiery end never counted as actual correspondence. Anything had to be better than that.

"Well, ah…" He stopped for a moment as emotions chased across his face, too rapidly to discern any of them. "I think my mom meant well. It started out with 'I'm so proud of you being in college' since neither one of my parents went to college, but then the letter sort dissolved into ranting really."

Maybe it wasn't so different from her mother's missives. "What do you mean?" The changing expressions said more than he did. None of them involved happiness, excitement, joy, or even the milder stepsister, contentment. "Tell me later,

I think your file is done." She nodded in the direction of his monitor.

Stella gathered up the notes for her work tonight. A jump drive saved what she'd already finished. Technically, she should be able to open the file back on her own laptop, although too many times, she discovered what should have worked often didn't. No reason to take chances. If she pushed it, she might get a few of her extra money assignments done.

The computer clock glowed 8:59 as Mitch powered down his computer, and she could hear Simon before he even opened the door.

Chapter Four

THE SQUARE CUBES that served as campus security lights threw down small pools of illumination at wide intervals leaving most of the surrounding in darkness. Small lights lined the path throwing a minimal light onto pedestrian feet, but not much else. They were a recent installation after a news story about sexual assault on college campuses. All it really managed to do was create even more shadows making almost everyone in a hoodie resemble a faceless serial killer.

Thank the Goddess that her colleague walked her to her door every night, a job that should have fallen to Cam.

Stella hooked her arm into Mitch's. "Let's do something fun for your birthday."

"Birthday was yesterday. You missed it." He covered her hand tucked into the crook of his arm with his. "What fun ideas do you have?"

Good question. It was a sizable campus with a variety of activities nearby. "We could go get a pizza, go bowling, even play miniature golf. Mainly, I just like to talk to you outside of work and class. We seldom get the chance, right?"

Despite her face turned up to his, she noticed two girls walking behind them. They rode the edge of their personal bubble eavesdropping. The two females whispered furiously. She didn't recognize them, but one looked a little familiar. She might have seen her somewhere earlier that day. Her head whipped back when she heard her name. The girls stopped, allowing them to move ahead on their own.

"Okay, sounds great. Let's turn here. I know a pizza place we can walk to." A warm breeze carried the aroma of car exhausts, fast food, and the sulfuric smell of a spent match.

"Think fast." A male voice shouted as a sputtering string of firecrackers landed near her feet.

Before she could even jump out of the way, Mitch swung her up into his arms and kicked the offending firework away. "Jerks. I ought to—" He growled the words.

Hoping to dampen what could be a fight, she added, "Get pizza," to the end of his sentence.

"You're right," he agreed before placing her feet back on the ground. "I worried that you'd get hurt."

Stella rather missed being in his arms, but she'd never mention it. Falling for Mitch, who was nice and protected her, would make her a lousy girlfriend. *It's more than Cam usually did.* Her troublesome-self whispered, always busy pointing out the flaws in her life. They walked a few moments in silence their hands no longer touching.

She touched his elbow just barely to get his attention. "You never finished telling me about the letter from your mother and why it was strange."

"Yeah, that." He sighed. "It started out okay with how proud she was that I was going to college. She went on to having a crappy job because she never went to college. Then on to dad dying and not even having an insurance policy and how hard her life has been ever since his death." He shoved his hands into his pockets.

"Whoa, that must have cheered you up immensely." How parents felt the need to burden their children with their own issues always amazed her. "Had the experience, myself. I get my own version of that from my mom." Her eyes rested on his wrists that ended in his pockets. She was willing to bet they'd gone into the pockets, eliminating the possibility of their hands casually touching.

Mitch pointed to the fairy lights draped over the trees outside the pizzeria. Stella knew the place, never actually went in, but was aware that it was a very popular hangout. A shiver of apprehension danced across her shoulders. No doubt, word that she'd been out dining with Mitch would ripple across campus. Not true, she was out with a friend celebrating a missed birthday. Of course, whether it mattered depended on *if* anyone knew she and Cam were an item.

The warm temperatures made the outside tables appealing. Stella settled back in the plastic lawn chair. The fairy lights illuminated the area with the help of a neon PIZZA sign and a votive candle flickering on each table for atmosphere. The striped table umbrellas advertised an Italian liqueur. A few couples huddled their chairs close together while conversing in low voices, no doubt, murmuring about how in love they were.

Every time the eatery's door swung open, groups of chattering students spilled out along with the sound of televisions turned to a sports channel while other students elbowed their way inside. The loud, boisterous voices indicated more than a few had too much to drink. Mitch pointed to a table farther away from the door in the shadow of a large tree. Without discussion, they both moved toward the table.

Mitch picked up a menu and flourished it. "Our location makes it impossible to read anything. I'll go in and order since I doubt as busy as they are they'll check to see if anyone is outside. Anything you don't want on your pizza?"

"None of those little fish things." She grimaced, thinking of tiny eyes staring at her while she bit into the slice. Yuk, it was enough to make her a vegetarian, but not quite.

Mitch laughed. "Got it. I don't like them, either."

His tall silhouette weaved around the other tables. How did anyone get service if the staff failed to look outside? A casual glance at the other tables revealed the whispering couples had no plates or pizza box on their tables. One couple had oversized sodas, but that could have come from the convenience store nearby.

The light from the open door had illuminated Mitch's profile briefly before he disappeared inside. Excellent sharp lines despite the glasses. Her father used to say a man's profile was his résumé. For some reason he believed those who had no inner purpose or character would be chinless individuals. Of course, his logic probably resulted from his own chiseled profile. In retrospect, considering how her father kicked her and her mom to the curb, a man's profile didn't mean squat.

A simmering spark of resentment flared. Just about the time, she thought she was over her father's desertion something happened, and the pain flared up again. Many middle-aged men abandoned their family when a younger woman beckoned. Often the younger woman ended up dumping the cheater, but it hadn't happened yet with her father.

Her lips pulled down as she crossed her arms and slumped into her chair. Mitch's shadow blocked out the surrounding light, as he leaned forward to look at her.

"Hey, what's wrong?" He slid into his seat, pulling it closer to hers. "I went inside and you were happy, but now you look like someone ran over your puppy."

Exhaling deeply, she pushed up in her chair and tried for a smile. Wasn't the whole purpose of the outing to cheer up Mitch who only got a lousy letter from his mother on his birthday? "I'm sorry. I'm not sure how it happened, but I started thinking about my father. I know I should be glad to have a father and all, but the way he left wasn't easy to deal with."

She reached for the votive candle, turning it in her hand, watching the flame flicker, almost die as the wax washed across it.

Mitch's larger hand pried the candle away from her. He positioned the candle closer to him before resting his hand on top of hers. "I know he left your mother for a younger woman. That's lame. How did this affect you?"

Her lips tightened, not wanting to tell the real story. "Of course, there were the endless arguments. I was the bone between the two of them. My mother pointed out how his selfishness would ruin my life. He'd scream back that she was the one who wanted children and he never did."

His hand tightened over hers. "Harsh. Did they know you overheard?"

Stella shrugged, not sure if Mitch could see the action in the dark. "I don't know. I doubt my father cared. He told me to my face that he'd never wanted children and I was the only reason he stayed in the miserable marriage as long as he did. In some convoluted way, I ruined his life, not my mother or him."

"Damn, that's hard."

Stella sighed heavily. "You're the only person I ever told, besides Leah, I mean. I would never tell my mother because that would set her off." The thought of her mother flying into a rage and threatening to drag her father back into court was a result she'd like to avoid. No good would come of it, especially if they wanted her to testify or something.

Even though it was dark, she knew Mitch was staring at her. His voice was soft when he asked. "You never mentioned it to Cam?"

An inelegant snort escaped her lips that she turned into a cough, pulling her hand from underneath Mitch's to cover it. *To think I almost said why would I tell Cam. Of course, you're supposed to tell your boyfriend all your personal issues.* She'd discovered a while ago that Cam didn't really listen. It wasn't too surprising. Her half-dozen high school dates weren't great listeners either, too busy trying to decide how they could get her into bed. Obviously, her father epitomized the disinterest men had for female problems.

"Um, no. I never told him. It never seemed like the right time."

It would have been the perfect time for Mitch to point out what a jerk Cam was, but he didn't. His silence made her wonder if it was due to pity for her over dating such a self-absorbed jerk or if he was bored with the whole conversation. Time to lighten things up. "Did you ask if you could get some birthday candles on the pizza?"

His silhouette reminded her of those black paper pictures her first art teacher enjoyed creating. At the time, Stella thought they all looked pretty much the same with the girls having ponytails and the boys with a few hairs sticking up awkwardly. Gazing at Mitch, she realized she'd be able to pick him out in dim light. Odd that she'd be able to do that. She hadn't really spent that much time observing him, despite work and their classes together, or had she?

His glasses slipped as he shook his head as if shaking off his silent stupor. A brush of his right hand pushed the glasses back in place. "I doubt this place has birthday candles. I didn't ask. I didn't want the fuss."

Didn't want the fuss. The words sounded artificial. It was something he probably thought he should say. Most people did want the attention even if it wasn't authentic. It made them feel special. Having a bunch of minimum wage employees interrupt their busy night to crowd around some stranger and force themselves to sing an off-key version of Happy Birthday was what he didn't want. Mitch wouldn't enjoy the curious looks of other diners wondering what was going on. Yep, she could do without that, too.

Still, it was hard to believe he did nothing for his birthday. "Do anything special for your birthday?" she asked, halfway fearing the answer. Back before her family life when into the toilet, her mother made the entire birthday week about her.

Instead of having her favorite food for one meal, it was a week full of delicacies such as cheeseburgers, ravioli, and little hot dogs in pork and beans. The last dish made her roll her eyes at her early culinary tastes. There were small gifts beside her plate all during her birthday week leading up to the big day.

Looking back, she could probably trace the disintegration of her family to the breakdown of birthday traditions. When she was fourteen, her mother seemed preoccupied about something and placed a candy bar by her breakfast setting instead of gifts, something her health conscious mother would have never done before. Because Stella was a big fan of sweet stuff, she gobbled the candy down with her cereal without comment, certain her mother would retrieve the bar. When she was fifteen, her mother forgot about her birthday until two days before the actual event and urged Stella to pick out her own gift, saying she'd pay for it. Her father didn't even make it home from a business trip that year in time for a lame birthday party with a handful of recycled candles on a frozen cake her mother hadn't thawed.

On her sixteenth birthday, her parents were deep into their fight mode. Her father was seldom home and argued with her mother behind closed doors when he did return. A two and a half inch wooden barrier didn't stop the words or the anguish from slipping under the door and wrapping itself around Stella. Neither one realized they'd both forgotten Stella's birthday. Thank goodness for Leah, who picked her up after a whispered call for help and ferried her back to her house. To her shock, Leah's family had decorated the house with a birthday banner and balloons. A cake with the correct number of candles graced the kitchen table. The memory brought tears to her eyes.

Mitch chuckled in a half-hearted way that caused her to shut down her own inner pity me show. It was far from a real laugh. That type of thing you do when you've done something stupid and there's no one to comment on how stupid it is, so you end up ridiculing yourself.

"Yeah, I threw a party."

Well, that didn't sound like the shy male she knew. "Really, who did you invite?" Part of her was miffed she wasn't invited, but she'd never admit it.

"Oh, the usual." He held onto the last word stretching it out. Holding up a fist, he began to count putting up his index finger. "There was me."

Well, she expected that.

His middle finger joined his second one. "Myself."

Oh, she knew where this was going. She wondered if she should stop him but didn't. He certainly had the right to feel sorry for himself.

His ring finger popped up. "The ghost of my father telling me how disappointed he was in me."

For a second, she wondered if his father's ghost did materialize. Stella believed in ghosts in theory but had never ever seen one.

His pinkie came up slowly. "Then there was my roommate's friend, I invited over for the night, without his knowledge, of course."

Roommate's friend and why would he invite this friend over without his roommate knowing. She knew Jake, his roommate, had a girlfriend because Mitch had mentioned the awkwardness of going back to his room and trying to pretend that they weren't doing it about six feet from his head. Dorm rooms were tiny unless you paid the extra two thousand to score a room in the newer dorms. Scholarship students never merited this.

She couldn't quite remember the name of Jake's girlfriend. It was a cutesy name. The type girls gave themselves like Candy, Treasure, or Precious. Did Treasure, or whatever her name was, cheer him up? Knowing Jake, Mitch was a definite step up, but still the thought made her uncomfortable. She wanted to ask but didn't. Instead, she folded her hands in her lap wishing there was something she could do.

Jumping to her feet, she announced, "I'll go check on that pizza." Suiting her actions to her words, she rushed to the door before he could say anything else. Inside, she worked her way through the crowd of standing students, wondering why they insisted on going somewhere that was so busy. The counter loomed in the distance rather like an oasis. Her goal was to get past the sea of half-drunk students, mostly male. No doubt a few would take the opportunity to grope her, one of the reasons she avoided crowded places. Inhaling deeply, she prepared to shoulder her way through the bodies with a few elbow jabs and sharp pinches for any gropers.

A bleary-eyed male a little taller than her turned to comment but stepped back allowing her to pass. He made sure to elbow the male next to him, who also stepped back. It was like the parting of the Red Sea. Of course, it would have to be renamed the parting of the drunken hoard. At the counter, she turned to see Mitch was right behind her with a fierce look on his face, daring anyone to touch her.

His expression shocked her. She'd never seen him look anything but friendly or thoughtful. Despite his leanness, his countenance promised retribution that even the most liquor-befuddled brain could process. Mitch was being protective. The idea thrilled her, sending a jolt of euphoria through her body. When was the last time a man protected her? It would have had to have been her father, but he'd quit defending her long ago.

It was probably politically incorrect to like the feeling, but she did. Mitch made the few steps to the counter and spoke close to her ear, "I told you I would get the pizza."

His earlier message never penetrated due to her rapid bolt before she fell victim to uncomfortable details of his self-made party the previous night. The smothering heat wafting from the pizza ovens and an excess of human bodies almost made her wish she stayed planted in the cooler outside air. Perversity caused her to shrug her shoulders. A deft move allowed Mitch to slip in front of her and signal the help. Stella grabbed the sodas while Mitch picked up the pizza and balanced it on his fingertips. Stella trailed behind her friend rather like a tugboat following a larger ship. It certainly was easier getting through the crowd. If she always had someone like Mitch by her side, crowds wouldn't be too bad.

Once they reached their outdoor table, she waited until they both sat before she launched her protest. "I told you this was my treat. It isn't much of a present if you pay."

Mitch opened the pizza box allowing a whiff of garlic laced

steam to escape. He pushed the open box in her direction. Picking up a piece, she brought it close to her mouth, but instead of biting, she spoke. "This isn't over, Mitch McDougall. Thought you'd trick me. Not sure why."

She bit into the melted cheese and tangy sauce enjoying the taste and warmth. Mitch grabbed a large triangle and folded it in half. Catching her eye in the dim light, he said, "You are the present."

"What was that supposed to mean?" With Cam, it'd mean he expected her to do something kinky he'd read about in a magazine or heard on that stupid radio show that the male half of the student body listened to faithfully. The show revolved around two adult men trading bathroom jokes and salacious stories similar to fourteen-year-old boys. Ironically, men believed their tales.

If she ever wondered who the smarter gender was, that show alone should make her feel superior. Mitch held up a finger as he chewed. Manners, so unexpected in a college student, but still appreciated.

Was he going to say something that would creep her out? Even if he had spent time with Treasure, she doubted he turned into a typical frat guy overnight whose twin obsessions were drinking and removing girls' thongs before they climbed on top of them.

Picking up his soda, he took a pull on the straw, probably helping the pizza go down. He set the drink down and touched the edge of her hand with his close fist. So gently, she almost wouldn't have felt it if she hadn't seen the action, reminding her of a butterfly kiss. Not exactly as if she experienced any of those, but what she thought one might be like.

"Being here with you is my gift. This is the first time I've been out with a beautiful woman since I started college."

"Seriously?" The whole idea was hard to believe. Mitch might not be a smooth-talking player, but hardly a troll. Her mouth twisted to one side, as she remembered most girls weren't hoping to score an intelligent male. Most preferred to be the smarter one. "C'mon, a guy like you could have any girl he wanted. Have you even asked anyone out?"

"Mmpft." The nonsense word was more of a reaction to having a mouth full of pizza and trying not to spit it across the table. Stella decided to take it as a *no. He hadn't asked anyone out.* A passing car's headlights brightened their corner of the terrace briefly, causing the groping couple to grumble, but spotlighted a tender expression on her companion's face that confused her.

His soft reply caused Stella to inch her seat closer to hear.

"College was never about parties or hooking up for me. I knew I'd have to hit the books to make it. Never really intended to do otherwise. I wasn't exactly a hit with the girls back at my old school, anyway. No fairy godfather bestowed on me the gift of irresistibility when I hit college, either. Besides the only girl, I really liked was involved with someone else. There really wasn't anyone else I cared about."

Out of the entire half-whispered conversation, she seized on one part. Mitch had a secret crush on a girl. Obviously, one with a boyfriend, but who could it be. The large lecture class, they both, attended was full of females, not that she paid attention to any of them. Her goal was to get there on time and take notes. He'd never talked to anyone, either. "Who's the girl? Maybe she's not very serious about the boyfriend. They could break up, ya know."

Here she was hoping for a couple to break up if it would make her friend happy. Couples split up all the time. Most were never together. They just hung out until someone more interesting caught their eye. A snippet of her earlier conversation with Cam slipped back and teased her with its implications. No, it couldn't be.

The flickering votive silhouetted Mitch's head and cast a tiny rosy circle on the plastic table. Enough light to see that the man angled his head away from her as he spoke. "I doubt they'd break up since she's planning on buying him a telescope for his birthday."

His words startled her almost as much as his resigned tone did. Sure, Cam hinted that Mitch liked her, but she dismissed it as one of his mind games. In Cam's mind, she gained more attractiveness if other men wanted her. Why it mattered if other men desired her baffled her since the man kept their relationship practically secret. The number of people who knew they were dating she could count on one hand. Cam, Mitch, Leah, and the cashier at the discount store where they shopped, but the last one may have assumed they were related since they were both blonde. Not sure, if it ever came up in conversation when Cam spoke to people.

At one time, she considered mentioning it. If Cam were someone else, she might have, but being acknowledged male eye candy on the campus made any mention bragging. After a while, she hesitated wondering if Cam shouldn't be the one advertising his hold over her. Her quandary about what terms to use for their relationship fell by the wayside with a constant barrage of classwork, work-study, and her side work of typing up lecture notes.

Mitch's abrupt mention of his own attraction to her caused her to blurt out, "Oh." She smashed her lips together sure she'd made a big stupid circle with her mouth.

Mitch's heavy sigh was louder than his words. "How could you not know?"

Easy, she wanted to answer, but she didn't. Memories of the endless thoughtful things Mitch did for her crowded her mind. He not only kept her caught up in class but put funny cartoons he'd cut out of the local paper on her desk. Half that time, he'd never known she was dating Cam. At first, she wasn't. Then, she was too unsure of Cam's player ways to admit to seeing him. When she finally did confess her infatuation to Mitch, there was a lull in their shared conversations and spontaneous gifts.

Had she been just using Mitch? Goddess, she hoped not. Would that make her little better than her mother, who her father accused of trickery. Her shoulders drooped as the pizza solidified into an uncomfortable mass in her stomach. "Why me? I'm not deserving of your affection."

Before he could answer, Stella stood to leave. Wiping away tears, she lunged away from the table, making an unsteady path through the tables.

A yelled comment about another chick who couldn't hold her liquor went right over her head until she realized the speaker meant her. She whirled, ready to face her nameless accuser and bumped into the solid form of Mitch.

He cupped her elbow and guided her onto the sidewalk. They had walked a few moments in silence before he spoke. "I didn't mean to upset you. I shouldn't have said anything."

More tears filled her eyes, threatening to fall. Was she crying for herself or Mitch? She wasn't terribly sure. "You didn't do anything wrong. It's me."

His hand tightened on her elbow as she stumbled on the uneven pavement. He kept her upright instead of allowing her to kiss the cement. "There's nothing wrong with you. I consider you perfect the way you are."

A grunt served as her reply. Even though it was a cliché, it was the first time anyone ever said it to her. One of the tears blurring her vision trickled down her face. Wouldn't it be wonderful to be that person he thought she was? "You don't know me that well, then."

"True," Mitch admitted. "But, I'd like to know you better."

What was that supposed to mean? Stella watched her feet as they negotiated the buckled sidewalk. "Better you don't. I kinda like the idea of you thinking so highly of me." Her words made her sound like a diva, so she managed to chuckle, making it sound like a joke. It wasn't.

She wasn't sure when it happened. The whole concept that she was broken and not okay. Maybe it was always part of her. After all, she had the nerve to show up nine months after her parents did the deed. Of course, her father enduring a loveless marriage as well as spending thousands of dollars on her upkeep didn't help either. Upkeep made her sound more like a lawn.

Her mother's newfound religion wasn't much better, which resulted in her mother always warning her of eternal damnation. This bothered her mom more than it did her since it somehow reflected poorly on her mother's parenting skills. She wasn't sure if the real problem was her going to hell or her mother looking like a less than a stellar parent. It might be both. Then, there was Kevin.

Oh, she tried not to think too much of the almost un-known senior who awkwardly asked her out to the senior prom. It was unfortunate he chose the morning her father stomped out of the house with a suitcase. The traumatic departure continued out on the front lawn where mothers with kindergartners stood on the sidewalk with strollers waiting for their oldest to board the bus.

Her mother clutched a skillet in her right hand because his abrupt announcement caught her in the middle of unloading the dishwasher. Her mother baited him by telling him that running back to his skanky ho would result in some incurable STD and a painful death.

The nearby mothers took a step back while covering their attentive children's ears. Those with more than one child had more of a challenge as far as ear coverage.

Her father, halfway in his car, yelled back. "You ruined my life. Everything you touch you destroyed." Catching sight of Stella, he added, "I wish you'd never been born."

Most people at the bus stop probably thought he was talk-ing to her mother. Apparently, that was the impression her mother received too, because she hurled the skillet at the car, dinging the door. Her father's face suffused with red, and he opened his mouth, but no words came out. Instead, he closed the car door and sped off.

Her mother, suddenly aware of her audience, dusted off her hands, announced to the listeners, "Good riddance." Her actions announced it was her plan to chase off her husband with a frying pan before work. Stella stayed on the front stoop staring at the departing car, knowing he'd been staring at her, wishing she'd never been born.

It was hard to stop thinking about it. So when Kevin Hardesty asked her if she'd go to the prom with him, she didn't answer, barely even heard the words as she turned away afraid she might start crying again. Apparently, not quickly enough, because it was all over school that the idea of going to prom with Kevin sent her into an enormous crying fit by the end of the day. When the gossip finally reached her via Leah, she wanted to find Kevin and explain. She never had the chance. He hanged himself that night from the local park swing set. The police found him near midnight when making their nightly rounds.

Though no note indicated he had killed himself due to her not going to prom with him, it didn't stop the rumors. Leah assured her she wasn't the problem. Bullying may have sent him over the edge. His stuttering made him an easy target. It also made it hard for him to ask her out, but he tried, and she cried. The image of her father screaming that she ruined everything she touched came to mind. Maybe he did mean her mother, then, but apparently, she was her mother's daughter.

They were almost at her dorm when she realized they had stopped talking while she fell into her memories and pulled the scabs off old wounds. "Sorry about being so quiet."

The lights were more plentiful around the building, illuminating the two of them. The majority of the campus pathways lights were close to the ground that shone only on feet. It never revealed people's faces or even those hiding near the path. Mitch was more than kind to walk her to her dorm.

His arms wrapped around her, holding her tight for a few seconds. The closeness and warmth cause a tickling sensation in the back of her throat. Oh, Goddess, she was going to cry some more, but instead of silent tears leaking out in the dark, it would be big ugly gasping cries. The thought made her break free of his embrace and dart for the entrance. She shoved past another girl opening the door, ignoring her muttered complaint.

Her rapid race up the stairs had her holding her side as she reached her own door. The sobs welled out as she swung open the door. No roommate in sight, which was good. She didn't want to explain why she was crying. It was hard to understand herself. Mitch considered her perfect, a definite improvement on her father's opinion.

Dropping to her bed, she pulled the covers over her not bothering to remove her shoes and cried.

CHAPTER FIVE

THE SOUND OF the door closing along with talking woke her. Stella blinked finding focusing difficult. Her fingers moved over her swollen eyes under the shielding covers.

A masculine voice she recognized as her roomie's current squeeze spoke. "Looks like ice queen tied one on. You said she was boring straight."

A snort, then a loud laugh rattled the room. How many people were in the room staring at her blanket-shrouded body?

"No way, she probably passed out from studying too much. I did hear a rumor she had a guy but never saw any sign of it."

"Looks like one person under the covers to me. Should I lift them to discover?"

Stella, curled in a fetal position, faced the wall holding tight to the polyester cocoon she had wrapped around herself. She squeezed her eyes shut to block out the brightness. Why couldn't she get a little privacy?

"Stop it." The hissed words pierced the mental fog enveloping her. "We're here just to get the weed and leave. Remember?"

A masculine mumble indicating nothing served as a response. A few footsteps and drawers opening and slamming, then a door shutting meant they were gone. Maybe. Stella counted to one hundred just to be safe. Slowly removing the blanket, she blinked in the glare of the light left on.

So straight, she was boring, huh? It wasn't a horrible thing to be. It sounded wrong, but there were worse things, such as getting kicked out of school for having drugs on the premises. Somehow, she'd have to get a new roommate. What excuse could she use without narcing out her roomie? Maybe she should use her roomie's excuse that she couldn't get enough studying done in her current environment. Hard for a college to argue against that one.

The swollen skin around her eyes pinched and stretched. Her face would be a mess tomorrow if she didn't use ice or even cold tea bags to take down the swelling. Standing, she stumbled in the direction of the small cabinet where she kept her food. Opening the door, she peered into the empty cabinet. "What the...?" Her surprise morphed into anger. Damn, another reason she needed a new roommate.

For the most part, she didn't have anything worth stealing, but apparently a box of breakfast bars, instant soup, and teabags must have disappeared with her visitors. Stella balled her hands on her hips. Probably just swept everything into a bag without even examining what they were grabbing. Difficult to imagine hot tea as a go to beverage to accompany the pot high munchies.

Pushing the door shut, she moved to the tiny fridge, not expecting too much inside. Stooping, she discovered a yogurt past its due date, a carton of takeout food that wasn't hers, and a tiny bottle of energy drink. None of it tempted her or was what she needed. She opened the even smaller freezer compartment for the two plastic ice trays. At least the ice would serve instead of the tea bags.

At last, something was going her way. She pulled out the first tray only to discover it was empty. "Seriously." She flung the tray toward her roommate's bed. Maybe the second one had ice in it. Her fingers lifted the light tray already knowing the answer before she tipped it up to the light. Empty.

The second tray followed the first as it flew across the room. Stella stumbled back to her bed. Too tired to do anything anyway. Tomorrow could be a mental health day. Goddess knows plenty of students took them. Mitch would cover for her at work, but she'd have to call him. The thought had her falling back on the bed.

How could she explain her bizarre behavior? The light was still on, but she didn't have the energy to turn it off. Rolling over, she freed her cover and pulled it over her, dimming the light. Tomorrow, she'd deal with everything.

Images of her impromptu date filtered into her dreams. *A white tablecloth stretched across the table with the absence of groping couples with their oversized plastic cups filled with who knows what made for a different scene. Mitch tucked his glasses into his shirt pocket as he smiled. His lips were moving, but she couldn't hear what he was saying. All she could see was how soft and inviting his eyes were as they came closer. She knew he was going to kiss her. The possibility tantalized as she leaned forward closing the distance the small table put between them.*

What type of kisser would he be? Music was playing in the background, the same trio of notes repeatedly, which sounded vaguely familiar.

"Answer your stupid phone!"

The strident command shocked Stella into wakefulness as her phone stopped chiming. An object landed on her covers. Lowering the blanket, she discovered her cell phone.

Palming it, she turned it to check who her persistent caller was. Cam, of course, just as well she didn't want to talk to him.

Her eyes flicked up to catch her roommate staring at her.

"Damn, you look like crap. What happened to you?"

Stella didn't need this. There was so much she wanted to say to her roommate but wasn't up to the confrontation. Instead, she walked past her to go to the bathroom. Living in the cheap dorms meant she had to share the facilities with a dozen girls.

Inside the restroom, she rested against the wall confronted with the fumes of a dozen different shampoos, body sprays, and styling agents. For females so concerned about looking good, they could trash a bathroom. Stella walked over to a mirror where the custodian had taped a note. In all caps, it read ITEMS LEFT OVERNIGHT WILL BE CONSIDERED TRASH. It was a familiar message that most of the students continued to ignore since it hadn't happened yet.

The tired face with red puffy eyes and pillow lines could have been used in an ad about the tribulations of college life. Despite the lack of alcohol, she looked hungover. Not that she had all that much experience partying hard, but she'd seen her share of dorm mates stumbling through the halls with smeared makeup and the acrid odor of vomit clinging to them. The only regret she had been acting the fool with her best friend on campus. She hadn't always considered Mitch that way, but there weren't a whole lot of contenders for the honor.

Resting one hand on her abs, she pushed her finger into the soft skin feeling for bloating. PMS might explain the emotional cascade she'd undergone, but not entirely. Her stomach felt surprisingly flat. Turning on the spigot, she splashed cold water on her face. It helped a little.

She swung the door closed on her bathroom stall the same time two residents entered.

"Did you hear about Stella being wasted?"

On her spot on the toilet, Stella stiffened in horror. They were talking about her. Any association with drugs would cost her scholarship. It was the driving reason she needed a new roommate. Knowing Cece, if administrators found weed in their room, she'd blame Stella, denying any drug use.

"Well, Emily did mention it. Didn't believe it. It's right up there with the story about her dating that hunk of man candy, Cam Winters."

The sound of pelting water accompanied their laughter. Realizing they were in the showers, Stella flushed, pulled up her pants, not even bothering to fasten them. She held onto them rather like would be gangsters who insisted on wearing jeans ten sizes too big. The door beckoned as she darted for it before the gossipers stepped out of the shower. Would they be embarrassed? All she knew was she didn't want to face anyone who felt a stoned Stella was more likely than boring Stella going out with Cam.

Students in the hallway served as obstacles for her to weave around. Biting her bottom lip, she offered up a short prayer that her roommate was gone as her hand touched the door-knob. The miracle of all miracles, she was. No way was she in any shape to attend class. Grabbing her computer, she shot an email to her professor explaining her absence as the stomach flu. It was something that usually never rated a doctor's note or a visit to the campus clinic. Unfortunately, it was also the one most hungover students used too.

Now, she'd have to call Mitch. She stared at her phone not wanting to make the call to explain. Instead, she texted, *Won't be at work. Cover for me. Thanks.* The phone chimed even before she could turn it off. A text from Mitch.

Are you avoiding me?

Well, yeah, she was avoiding him and everyone else on the planet. Mentioning it would invite more questions. What could she say? The idea of going away to a secluded spot in the woods without everyone speculating about her behavior appealed. She'd already informed her prof she had the flu. Mitch would probably take an extra handout in class for her if there were any. A chance conversation might occur with Dr. Fleming mentioning she had the flu. With all the possible outcomes, she needed to stick with the same lie.

No, of course not. I just have the flu.

That should satisfy him. He might tell her feel better, which was the favorite catch phrase when a person announced illness. It always sounded more like an order. You feel better.

The underlying message was sick people are no fun. Get well or I'll drop you as a friend. Maybe it only sounded that way to her. Could be she was overthinking it. The phone chimed again.

You didn't act sick last night, A little moody, but not sick.

Sweet Goddess save her from intelligent men. The impulsive plea horrified her. *I didn't mean it. Don't rescue me from smart men.* Outside of Mitch, there had been a void of smart men in her life. It could be that hormones trumped intellect every time, even though all the males must have received reasonable grades for admittance. Their bizarre fraternity initiations, beer pong, and dares to bed as many females as possible didn't symbolize higher learning in any form. More than a few had convoluted plans to cheat their way through the year.

Moody, huh. He got that right. Nothing she wanted to deal with right now. She considered not replying, but that would have the considerate male stopping by to make sure she hadn't rolled out of bed gaining a concussion in the process. Argh, what to do? Her fingers tangled in her hair as she shoved a restless hand through her tresses. What a mess. The phone chimed again.

I'm coming over. I'll get you some chicken soup from the shop on the corner.

Her lips tilted up. He was a thoughtful man. The prospect of his arrival catapulted her out of bed. He couldn't come over. It would be hard to fake an illness with him there. Full sunlight filtered through the cheap blinds indicating late morning. A glance out the window revealed students heading to class, which she should be. Guilt rode her hard rather like one of those demons her mother continually insisted were hitching a ride on her. Apparently, demons were not big fans of walking since they were always busy hitching a ride on someone. There had to be some way to discourage Mitch. A little truth sometimes works.

> *I lied. It's my period. The cramps are super bad. Don't come over. Nothing you can do. Probably hate you because you're a male and don't have to go through this.*

Periods, cramps, tampons all worked on men similar to how a cross did on traditional vampires. The idea grossed out the males, in general, since their bodies never offered up monthly gifts of blood. At the most, men knew they couldn't offer any helpful advice. Most usually clammed up or changed the subject. Would Mitch be any different?

> *Understood*

Obviously, he was the clam up sort. Her stomach lurched. All her talk of flu might be having undesirable consequences. Then again, it could be the lack of food. Maybe she should have let Mitch bring her soup.

Her tummy gave another rumble. The clever thing would be to get cleaned up and go to the meal hall. If nothing else, she could probably get some fresh fruit and a granola bar. Breakfast would be over by the time she got there. Especially, since a shower was a must with her Medusa locks. Of course, that meant interacting with people.

Stella stumbled back to her bed and sat. Her shoulders drooped as she considered all she had to do. "Goddess, I can't handle it." Even eating required too many steps. Turning off her cell phone, she climbed back under the covers. The only good thing about her roommate was Cece would leave her alone and make no annoying efforts to see if she were still alive.

Sleep came fast, taking her under. She tumbled off her wakefulness boogie board and slipped into the ocean of sleep. Generally, she fought her descent into slumber, but not today. Her last conscious thought consisted of wondering why anyone would fight sleep. It was such sweet mindless place devoid of reality and the associated responsibilities.

A brownish mist circled around her feet. Dead trees decorated the landscape, throwing out long, black ragged shadows. No moon or sun in the cloudy sky made her question the shadows. The flapping wings of a bird drew her gaze upward. A raven or possibly a crow landed on a nearby tree.

The bird's dark eyes fixed on her. Most people considered the crow a symbol of death. Then again, in folklore any bird in the house indicated a future death, probably because a bird in flight represented the soul. Stella kept her gaze fixed on the bird trying to remember the most positive symbolism for the large bird.

Crows were highly adaptable and intelligent. Shamanic meanings included being fearless, magic, personal transformation, even destiny. For the most part, all good things, her mood lightened a little. Several other crows lighted on the tree, crowding it with their dark bodies. The birds shifted on the branches making room for new arrivals.

What did an entire flock of crows mean? Murder was the weird term for a group. The crow also served as a trickster in animal legends. Was it an elaborate con? If it were, she was clueless. What if the birds were ravens? All she could think of was Edgar Allan Poe's poem with the raven answering "Nevermore." In the end, she couldn't quite remember the entire poem. Just that something about a depressed writer whining about his dead true love. She wasn't sure if the raven's Nevermore was telling him he'd never love again or what.

One of the birds cawed, causing the others to caw, flapping their wings until suddenly the tree lifted off the ground.

"Stella, Stella, I know you're in there." The male voice penetrated along with the pounding she thought at first was the sound of the tree carried away by countless crows.

Wakefulness trickled in slowly. The weave of the blanket filled her view; making her wonder if it was the sky. The cloudy brown sky turned a nauseating puke green. The pounding continued. A part of her knew she should investigate, but another part voted for ignoring it. Didn't things go away when you failed to acknowledge them? Pulling the blanket closer, she rolled toward to the wall and away from the sound.

"Stella, open this door or I'm going to the campus police!"

Police. Her eyelids snapped open. There was a reason she wanted to avoid the cops, but she couldn't remember why. Definitely would have to answer the door. Eventually, she might remember the thing about the police. A groan escaped as she pushed into a sitting position. The blanket served as her protective shield as she half draped it over her head and across her shoulders. A combination stagger-stumble walk brought her to the door. Blinking several times, she tried to shake off the last vestige of the crow dream.

It might be Mitch with food. Buoyed by the hopeful thought, she threw the door open. A scowling Cam greeted her. What was he doing here? Her memory might be lagging some, but she was sure she as much as broke up with him when he suggested using her job to do some grade changing.

Cam's eyes took a downward sweep of her body and then returned to her face before speaking. "You look like shit!"

Her hand still on the doorknob propelled the door shut before the thought even solidified in her brain. Unfortunately, Cam's upraised hand stopped the door just short of closing. Her moment of indecision gave him enough time to push his way into her room.

Stella took a step back, sliding away from him. This was the man she loved? Did love? The angry male placed his hands on her shoulders and burned her with another disapproving stare. "God, you're a mess. I came over here to prevent you from doing anything else foolish."

Foolish? She backed away the way a person would from a rattlesnake. Did she even know him? The back of her legs hit her bed, destroying her balance and sending her windmilling backward. As soon as she hit the mattress, she scrambled back to her feet. No reason to send the wrong signals. Although right now, his sneer reflected the mattress dance was not under consideration.

He folded his arms and leaned back against the door. "I guess I shouldn't be too surprised you look like garbage. That's what happens when you go slumming."

Okay, she'd give a zombie a run for her money as far as looking like death five days old. The mirror already delivered the unwelcome news. What was this slumming nonsense? Sure, the college town might not be affluent, but it was no ghetto either.

Cam continued talking, not waiting for her reply. "You thought I wouldn't hear about you and Mitch's date the last night?"

Stella almost corrected him but decided against it. Sure, it wasn't a real date, but no need to tell him that, especially since it upset him so much. It was probably the most emotion she'd seen from the man when he wasn't watching sports channel. Could Cam be jealous? His face grew flushed as he spoke.

He did come all the way to her dorm to see why she wasn't taking his calls. As for the disbelieving shower girls, she hoped they caught a glimpse of him. The furrow in his forehead smoothed out as he flashed his potent smile. His lips were moving again. Stella shook her head to clear it. His voice had an echoing quality similar to being in a tunnel. Slowly, she deciphered the words.

"I'll give you thirty minutes to get ready. Then, I'll swing back by and pick you up."

Cam was taking her somewhere. Where? "Are we going out to eat?" Crossing her fingers on one hand, she certainly hoped so.

"Lunch usually involves food." His lips twisted as he shook his head. Two long steps took him to the door. "Thirty minutes."

The door closed leaving Stella frozen for a few seconds. "Thirty minutes!" She grabbed her shower caddy, a maxi dress, underwear, and a towel. She sprinted to the showers. The row of bathroom mirrors reminded her from various angles how horrendous she looked.

The showers started out cold, which meant a twenty-second warm up period to make the water bearable. No time today, stepping into the icy water set her teeth chattering. Tensing her muscles, she endured it. Besides, it would help her shake off the lethargy. The sense of despondency that had fastened itself to her required extra loofah scrubbing. Call it exfoliating, but she was trying to rid herself of the feeling that nothing mattered.

The bathroom door opened, and two girls came in talking. Stella didn't recognize the voices, but that wasn't too surprising. A full schedule, work, and Cam kept her too busy for the social activities that might have gained her a few friends. Then again, she didn't have a whole lot of use for girls who only cared about boys, nail polish, sex, and shoes. Part of her wanted to warn them not to depend on men to fulfill them, using her mother as a poster child of what happens when a woman expects a man to make her dreams come true.

That type of behavior would make her a social pariah if she weren't already. Fingers in her hair, she lathered up. Ready to step back into the water flow for the rinse, she stopped when she heard Cam's name.

"Cam Winters was in our dorm. I can't believe it. I didn't think he made personal visits because girls just line up outside his apartment." Laughter greeted the remark.

Her teeth ground together as she imagined the speaker falling into a sinkhole that opened up underneath her. Her fingers continued to lather her hair as she continued to eavesdrop. How did they know he had an apartment as opposed to a dorm room? Ugly answers she didn't care for crowded her mind.

"The man must be desperate if he's knocking on dorm room doors." The females found this remark equally hilarious.

The sound of the door slamming indicated another woman entered. Stella stepped under the stream of water still able to hear their laughter and catch a word here and there. Her curiosity propelled her out of the water again. Conditioner, she needed to condition her hair. Time was ticking. Cam would probably be back in exactly thirty minutes too. It would help if gossip girl and friend cleared out, allowing her some peace.

An extra big glop of conditioner landed in her hand. Good. It would make her hair look greasy in a couple of days, but the extra conditioner would make her hair shine today. She needed something after the mess Cam witnessed. It was no wonder he didn't kiss her goodbye. Instead, he slipped out of the door like a cat burglar.

A third voice joined the gossip crew. It sounded somewhat familiar, but she couldn't place it.

"Sex is the last thing Cam would be here for. The man could stand naked on a corner and be mobbed by women who wanted to blow him."

The words made her want to vomit, but luckily, her empty stomach didn't comply. Sure, Cam turned heads with his underwear ad-worthy physique, sun-streaked hair and knowing smile, but still. Did the women on campus have no dignity? Her fingers slowed smoothing conditioner to the ends of her hair. Did she have no dignity? She and Cam had a relationship. Wasn't he taking her out? He certainly hadn't done that in a while. A grocery trip to the discount mart did not count as a date.

"I heard he was flunking out of most of his classes and even got Hilary to do his homework for economics, but found out she only looked smart."

The trio chuckled, then, went on to discuss their plans for the day before heading for the showers or toilets. The breakup of the group had Stella shimmying the maxi dress over her still wet body with no time to dry off or shave her legs. She needed to be gone before the girls popped out of the various stalls. Why was she running? She'd done nothing wrong. Inhaling deeply, she tried to calm down her racing heart. Any other girl would brag about Cam taking her out for lunch. Instead, she acted as if she were on some spy mission. No reason she shouldn't go out. She was as good as the rest of the females on campus. Her bold affirmation did little to convince.

A clear path greeted her as she poked her head out of the shower enclosure. A quick tooth brushing was all she'd allow herself before heading out. Makeup and hair she'd do in her room. With any luck, her roommate wouldn't be there.

In her room, she set her travel alarm clock in front of the

mirror. In and out of the shower in under ten minutes, but she didn't shave. She forgot her shower shoes too. That wasn't like her. Mitch occasionally teased her about her lists and obsessive organization. Her purple shower shoes were still in the caddy. Great, now she'd probably get athlete's foot or some other fungal bacteria.

Brush in one hand and blow dryer in the other, she smoothed out her natural blonde hair. The heat flushed her face, but even considering that the mirror reflected back an attractive woman. If she owed her parents nothing else, they were both reasonably good-looking, which was probably the reason her father found it so easy to hook up. If Cam were only in the market for looks, then she'd fit. Hundreds of other girls on campus would too.

She shook her eyeliner, trying to decide if she'd go with a clean line or a little Cleopatra curve on the end. Straight line, she didn't have time to risk the curve and starting over when it smeared. What was so different about her that had Cam continually asking her out until she accepted?

A quick swipe of mascara finished her eyes. She fluttered them at her reflection lightening her mood a little. She could almost admit that Cam was dating her for sex, which wouldn't be too different from most males on campus. While that might be true, he could easily date women, hotter and better in the sack than she was.

The blush brush whisked over both cheeks, and a smear of lightly tinted lip-gloss finished her makeup. Could it be true about Cam flunking? She never could accuse the man of studying too much. The only sign of grade anxiety was when he asked her if she were capable of changing his grades. His argument sounded logical with the prospect of losing his scholarship, but as his girlfriend, her job should be to encourage him to study and bring his grades up, not help him cheat.

Her phone chimed the same time she gave her hair a final flip. Picking it up, she scanned the screen.

Thirty minutes are up. Waiting downstairs, outside.

Stella's eyes drifted back to her travel clock. Two minutes remained, but she wouldn't quibble. Instead, she grabbed her purse and headed out. Waiting outside meant none of the catty girls would see Cam escort her. On the other hand, she didn't have to do his homework, either, to score a date.

The tiny voice that she sometimes labeled *mother* whispered, "If you change his grades, he'd be yours forever." The idea was tempting. Sure, Cam wasn't the greatest boyfriend, but it was certainly better than being alone, wasn't it? Her sandals made a clopping sound as she hurried down the stairs. The stupid elevator took forever, forcing her into the dank stairwell that hung onto smells the way a dog guards a bone. The combined aromas of pizza, vomit, and body spray caused her to cover her mouth with her hand as an impromptu mask.

Her steps slowed as she approached the first floor. Cam should be outside the door waiting for her. Possibly leaning against the tree where all the disbelieving residents could see him. *Yeah, that's right. Bookish Stella hooked one of the campus hot bodies.* Today would be a great day. Obviously, the man was going to make their relationship more public, more real. Her lips lifted in an impromptu smile. The depression that had embraced her in a chokehold and held her down under waves of despair last night vanished as she faced the front door.

The majestic oak trees that provided shade and trysting spots for young lovers gave the dorm's façade collegiate charm. Her lips twisted as she recalled the college pamphlet. Yep, that sucker had all the marks of a PhotoShop expert. Of course, at the time, she didn't care about the campuses appearance. All she knew was that she wanted out of the battleground her home had become and a full scholarship was the ticket.

A few students stood in the tree shadows. No Cam anywhere near the building. A quick tap brought her phone back to life and allowed her to reread Cam's message. If he was waiting, where was he? A breeze ruffled the dress around her ankles, cooling the damp sections that stuck to her body. Absentmindedly, she pulled the dress away as her eyes scanned the area. Two short toots of a car horn caught her attention.

The sound came from the side parking lot almost empty except for a handful of cars. Usually, parking space rated up there with premium concert tickets during midweek. The weekends were different since most students did their best to get away even if it meant visiting another college or driving home. Most managed to entertain themselves with the limited attractions of movies, restaurants and glow golf. A few used the weekends to run those former mom errands of laundry and grocery shopping.

The lack of cars made it easy to spot Cam's familiar red car. It looked more like a garish Easter egg to her, but he insisted it was an Italian sports car, an ancient one. Her hand went up in greeting as she hurried to meet him. Instead of getting out and greeting her, he stayed in the car. As she drew closer, she noticed he sported sunglasses.

It was almost as if he was hiding, and the sunglasses were part of his disguise. Stella squashed the suspicious thought as she hurried toward the car. It was a sunny day, which meant anyone would wear sunglasses. Yeah, that was it.

Chapter Six

"GOOD, YOU'RE HERE." Cam glanced in his rear view mirror before reversing. Stella kept quiet, busy fastening her seat belt. It clicked in place about the same time Cam floored it. The small car had lurched before the power kicked in, hurtling it down the narrow road. They careened onto the main road causing another car to swerve out of their way. Stella closed her eyes, sure of impending death. A honk, muttered curses, and Cam laughing assured her she lived instead of waiting a soul assignment in Summerland. Somehow, she forgot Cam's driving habits since her trips in his car were rare. *Wouldn't want people to see the two of them together.* Stella shook her head trying to rid it of the annoying inner voice. Why did her conscience develop such a cynical attitude?

"I heard that." Cam's head swung in her direction. The dark lenses hid his eyes, but his lips pressed together in a firm line. "How many times do I have to tell you this is a high-performance engine? I have to rev it up occasionally. Can't drive around like your eighty-year-old grandmother."

Instead of pointing out, she didn't have a grandmother; she watched the scenery fly by. Strange, he never remembered.

She'd mentioned it more than once. Her mother's parents died in a bizarre safari accident. Her father lost contact with his parents, which left her with no grandparents to fuss over her.

Groups of students in school T-shirts and colored face paint stood near the bus stop. There must be a game. The light changed, forcing Cam to slam on the brakes, propelling Stella forward until the seat belt locked, throwing her back into the seat.

The stop allowed her more outside world observation. A couple holding hands strolled in the direction of the bus stop. The tall, slender male angled his head toward the girl. His nod and subsequent smile were indicative of his attentiveness to his date. The girl tiptoed to kiss his cheek. The spontaneous display made her envious. Why couldn't she and Cam be more like that?

Lunch out was a start. In the end, she wasn't the type of female who inspired whole-hearted affection. Goddess knows her mother wasn't one either. The stiffness of her parents' relationship hadn't been evident until she started hanging out with Leah. At first, Leah didn't invite her over, preferring to meet her at other places. It made Stella think that her parents were even worse than hers were. The natural affection between Leah's parents, Adam, and Maura, surprised her since she believed married people stopped touching around the age of thirty or whenever they had kids.

The last thing she wanted to be was forty plus years old throwing things at her husband's car as he drove out of her life. Her eyes cut to Cam without thought. The smirk gracing his face wasn't for her. A more charitable person would call it a smile. It wasn't.

The way he drove with his shoulders back and his smug expression demonstrated he'd taken in his current surroundings and found no one nearby that he considered in his league. A tidbit of information from psychology class about people accepting or rejecting people in five seconds popped in her head. Something about a casual glance decided if a person was helpful, dangerous, or not necessary. At some point, Cam decided she was helpful.

Yeah, helpful, it wasn't what she wanted. She didn't expect some awe-inspiring love where a man would travel to the ends of the Earth to rescue her, but something a little better than being helpful. In some ways, she was little more than a maid service with side benefits. Still, he was taking her out.

The car picked up speed as they left the congested campus area. Stella studied the strip malls, churches, and an assortment of neighborhoods. Not having a car kept her close to the school. The scarlet and golden tree leaves hinted at a season change despite summer heat lingering past its time. The buildings became less and less as browning cornfields dominated the scenery, out of the city and its associated chain restaurants.

"Where are we going?"

Cam kept silent for a few heartbeats. For the tiniest moment, a scenario rolled out where he dumped her dead body in a ditch. Fear ran down her arm raising the hairs in the process. *Stop being stupid. He has no reason to kill me. Haven't witnessed a crime. Have nothing worth taking. In this case, I'm one of those people who's worth more alive than dead. The* sudden crime scene images faded with his reply.

"There's a diner this way I thought would appeal to you since it's small town and all."

Small town? She'd never mentioned being from a small town, a city, not an overly large city, but not a small town, either. He was confusing her with someone else, not a flattering thought.

"Oh." Not the best response, but considering everything swirling around in her brain, it had to be the safest.

A few left-hand turns onto narrow roads with almost no traffic demonstrated Cam knew the way. He may have known it because he'd been there before. An abandoned double-wide with a rusted truck chasis resting on cinder blocks marked the turn. Who lived there once? Better yet, why did they leave? The obvious answer would be better prospects somewhere else, rather like her father. Maybe the air inside the doublewide bore the taint of contempt and disappointment too, although, right now, it probably smelled of mold, mildew, and decay.

Why do people promise to love one another and then leave, after doing unspeakable damage? Of course, there may have never been any love between her parents, just a small flare of attraction mistaken for the real thing. How did a person know when they were in love? All she had to do was stand still for five seconds in the dorm lobby and she'd hear a girl announce her love for a current boyfriend. If she stood a few seconds longer, another girl would publicly plot revenge against someone she used to love. As words went, love got passed around more than a bottle of Jack. Women who barely tolerated one another kissed the air near each other while trilling their affection, barely waiting for the other to leave before ridiculing her.

Trust was a much harder word to earn. Few people believed in one another. Her eyes cut to Cam. Nope, she didn't trust him. Wished she could, but so far had no real reason to. If she could trust him, then maybe she could love him, but to do any of that she'd have to get to know him. It hadn't happened yet. The fact she never knew about his journeys to the country for small town dining epitomized how little he shared.

A small diner with a neon sign with a burnout N announced it *DI ER*, which sounded rather unappetizing. Underneath the neon, a narrow strip of plywood declared *Good Eats Inside* in sloppy blue painted letters. An older pickup truck and a dated sedan covered with religious bumper stickers sat in front. Cam drove across the pitted, gravel parking lot slowly and parked alongside the truck.

"We're here." He grinned at her, similar to announcing a glorious event.

Now, she didn't expect white tablecloths and tuxedoed waiters, but something more than this. Road Kill Café might serve as an alternate name or the 50/50 diner because you had a fifty percent chance of getting food poisoning. Stella had sat in the car for a second, before she noticed Cam standing in front of the car. Oh yeah, she needed to get out. If Cam liked the restaurant so much, it must be good. Her forced smile stretched her lips upward, but no joy inhabited it.

The hum of insects greeted her as she opened the car door. Black flies swirled in some abstract landing pattern before swooping down into the bed of the truck. Curiosity pulled her feet closer to the truck bed. Inside lay a buck with molting antlers. Congealed blood covered the area around the bullet hole hosting dozens of flies. The glassy, dead eyes stared at her, importuning her, asking her why.

A small shriek and a jump backward served as her only response to the unvoiced question. Cam laughed at her, making her wonder if he parked by the truck deliberately. Perhaps, he'd already seen the deer inside. Her excitement about their date had fizzled when she realized they weren't eating in town. Died a little more when she saw where they were, and she wasn't too sure if any enthusiasm survived.

"C'mon, let's go. I'm hungry." Cam gestured to the diner, probably hoping to hurry her.

Her feet moved, but she'd left her appetite back in the truck with the deer. Once she reached Cam, he draped an arm around her shoulders, which improved her mood somewhat. His hand cupped her shoulder and brought her in for a squeeze. "You're my girl, right?"

The words both cheered and puzzled her. Sure, last night, she had doubts if she wanted to be Cam's girl, especially if he wanted her to do things that went against her personal code of ethics. Today, though, after hearing those girls doubt that Cam could be interested in her. She wanted to be his girl, but a keen desire to parade him in front of the doubting Thomasinas didn't qualify as a reason for a relationship.

He squeezed her against his side, his fingers pressing down on her upper arm. "I didn't hear your answer."

It hurt. She'd probably have finger-shaped bruises tomorrow. "Yeah, I am," she muttered the words while working her shoulder trying to shake off his grip. He relaxed his hand, allowing it to ride lightly against her upper arm. It must have been a mistake. Forgot his own strength, that's all.

A cowbell clanged as the door opened. A tired, middle-aged woman attired in a garish orange smock paused in her discussion with the two camouflage-garbed hunters. "Hey, be with you in a minute."

Half dozen booths comprised the seating. Cam chose one closest to the jukebox. The waitress bustled to their booth as soon as they sat, placing paper napkin wrapped utensils along with paper mat menus on the table.

The woman cracked her gum, before grinning at Cam. "Haven't seen you in a while, last time you were with that cute little…" She stuttered to a stop and glanced at Stella, before finishing. "…cousin."

Yeah, cousin. Stella wasn't buying. Apparently, she wasn't the only girl he'd driven to the isolated diner. It made her wonder how long a while was. It could be two months, two weeks, or even two days if—she glanced at the server's nametag—if Doreen was teasing. Not feeling any specialness. Wasn't being someone's girl supposed to feel different?

Cam settled for the Hungry Man platter. The bacon double cheeseburger with fixing's, French fries, onion rings, and hush puppies should not only fill him up but also give him indigestion. Her salad order received a censorious look from Doreen. Stella's desire to eat any meat had died when she spotted the buck. The grim line of the server's lips announced her oddity by not ordering something fried. No way could she explain how the deer's eyes made her reconsider her eating habits, at least for a day.

Order tucked into the pocket of her bright smock, the woman started the burger on the grill. Apparently, the place was a one-woman operation. It explained why she remembered Cam. Didn't look like the place merited too many customers.

Cam reached across the table, grabbing her hand that rested on the paper menu. "I know it doesn't look like much, but the food is good. It can be our place."

Yay.

He flashed his usual grin, before releasing her hand and sliding across the vinyl bench seat. She thought he might be moving to her side, which would be somewhat romantic. He stood and headed for the jukebox. He dropped in change and punched a selection before turning back to her. "It only seems right that we have our own song."

A bell when off somewhere in her heart, but that could have been the fries alarm, too. The man was trying. The rich, mellow sounds of The Temptations singing *My Girl* filled the diner, causing the two hunters to glance back at them.

One chuckled, while the other commented, "Yeah, I used to be an operator like that. Had all the girls swooning."

Cam held out his hand to her. He wanted to dance, right here in public, in the tiny area running in front of the booths. Okay. She put her hand in his and stood. He placed one hand on her waist and held her hand as they slowly box stepped around the room. She sighed a little, as he brought her closer. Close enough for her to rest her head on his shoulder.

When other girls were picking out prom dresses, her family disintegrated in full view of the neighbors. No time for romantic moments, especially with her entire attention focused on getting scholarship-worthy grades. Even though they were dancing cheek to cheek in the middle of nowhere, it still reigned as one of her best dances. A faster song came on, sending them both back to the table.

Cam shrugged as he sat. "Jukebox is some relic from the sixties. All they have are ancient songs."

Did that mean *My Girl* wasn't their song? It could mean that was the closest he'd come to expressing his feelings, and then again, he'd probably never heard it before. Most people didn't have a mother like hers. Before her religious conversion, her mother played the oldies station aloud and sang along energetically. In retrospect, her singing reflected the state of the marriage. Whenever her parents fought, her mother's singing lacked energy, or she'd only sing the angry girl songs. Near the end, she'd quit singing altogether. Occasionally, she'd whispered the lyrics to a melancholy song. Stella knew something was wrong then, but pretending she didn't was easier.

Doreen arrived with their food, placing a large steaming platter in front of Cam. The grease glistened under the fluorescent light turning Stella's stomach a little. The plastic bowl the server shoved in front of her barely merited the name salad. Strips of American cheese covered the wilted lettuce, without another vegetable in sight. As an afterthought, Doreen placed a bottle of ranch dressing on the table, not asking what she wanted. Ranch might have been all they had since it didn't look like the type of place to attract healthy eaters.

Cam bit into his cheeseburger with enthusiasm. Picking up her fork, she stabbed at hers, forcing herself to swallow the slimy cheese and overly salty meat. The appeal of the place must be the absolute assurance you'd never run into anyone you knew. The location would suit drug dealers, as well as men who were into secret dating. Then again, Doreen would remember whoever came in.

Between the burger and fries, Cam hesitated long enough to speak. "Did you think about what we talked about?"

"What did we talk about?" Her fork loaded with week old lettuce hesitated on its way to her mouth. Sure, she thought about it. Hoped he'd forget the whole idea.

Another record dropped in the machine. The Supremes crooned about *Baby, Where Did Our Love Go*. She had to wonder if Cam picked the records in any particular order. If not, then Fate must have taken a hand in the serendipitous placement. Her expectations of today being an incredibly romantic day showed what a gullible fool she could be.

"You know." He gestured with a fry. "The grade changing to keep my scholarship. Got some friends that need grade changing too. Six of them."

Her fork dropped from her hand, pinging against the table and drawing an annoyed glance from Doreen.

"Something wrong with your salad?" The server snarled the words daring her to complain.

"No nothing," Stella squeaked, causing the hunters to chuckle.

"Yeah, that one has no backbone," Doreen told the hunters

loud enough for Stella to hear. "Not like the redhead."

Part of her tried to track the conversation while the rest of her wrestled with the scope of the outrageous suggestion. She picked up her fork stalling. "Six friends, really?"

"They're on scholarships too." Cam explained as he bit into an oversized onion ring.

Yeah, and they probably partied hard never considering the consequences. "I don't think it can be done. One person, maybe, but Financial Aid makes quarterly checks. You can't have a D, and then finish with an A."

Cam stopped eating; his eyes rolled upward. He rubbed the bridge of his nose with his index finger. "Don't give me an A, but something high enough that it averages out to a 2.5. That's all I need to keep my scholarship."

"Why should I do this?" Never mind that she did not intend to do so.

The music changed again to *Eleanor Rigby*, a Beatles tune about a lonely woman no one cared about, especially poignant lyrics. Could it be her life story?

"Looks to me like you're getting real chummy with Mitch. Did you know he has a DUI?"

Mitch defined straight arrow.

"I can tell by that look on your face you don't believe me. Go ask him. Back in the summer, in Michigan. Apparently the awards board doesn't know, or he wouldn't have received a scholarship."

Her heart sank as the Beatles sang about all the lonely people. It gave her a sudden desire to kick the machine. The worn record caught, repeating, "Nobody came." What little she knew of Mitch's life, he probably thought nobody cared, especially with a father who checked out by dying and a mother who blamed him for the death.

This must be how a cornered rat feels. Sure, she could call Cam's bluff. The jerk made it up. An emotional push into the direction he wanted her to go. She shoved the salad bowl away from her, unable to stand looking at it for one more second. Cam's smug face made her doubt Mitch's innocence. Strange, it hadn't popped up yet. A misspelled name or a wrong number on a social could bury a file. It also might explain why Mitch worked so hard at the work-study job and classes. He had to get as much done in as little time as possible.

Doreen interrupted the silence. "Oh lookee, you gobbled down that hungry man platter. I do love a man with an appetite." She giggled girlishly. "Maybe a piece of pie might fill the hole you got."

The woman leaned over the table exposing her generous cleavage as she picked up the platter. Stella stood abruptly. "Excuse me." She headed for the door marked restrooms. The woman could crawl all over Cam as far as she cared.

Raw plywood created a makeshift stall around a cracked seat toilet. A chipped mirror reflected back her shocked expression. Oh yeah, no surprise there. She thought today would be super romantic. Instead, she ended up holding a friend's future in her hands. She could save Mitch's life if she forfeited her own aspirations. Then again, maybe, she could get away with it. Leah would know what to do. She typed in Leah's number into her cell and then held it up to her ear.

No ringing. A glance confirmed what she suspected, no

bars. Of course, there wouldn't be anything as practical as cell service in the middle of nowhere. Goddess, she had to get out of here. Placing the phone back in her purse, she rested her hands on the sink. What was she going to do?

A twist of the faucet sent water spilling into the bowl after an initial protest from the pipes, sounding like no one had made use of the bathroom in quite a while. If they did, they hadn't used the sink. Disgusting. The water flowed clear and cold after a few seconds of rust. Good. A few splashes helped combat nausea that the questionable salad and suspicious request had on her. Mascara pooled around her eyes, running in rivulets down her cheeks. Yeah, she looked the way she felt.

It didn't matter anymore how she looked for Cam, but she wouldn't give Doreen another ridicule opportunity. A damp paper towel removed most of her makeup. Inhaling deeply, she considered what she knew, which wasn't much. No decisions should rest on so little information. The reflected, slightly damp, female stared back waiting for an answer, a solution. "I need to get back."

Chin up, shoulders back, she marched out of the restroom only to find Cam talking to Doreen as he shoveled down apple pie. Doreen perched one hip on the wall separating the booth from the work area. She leaned forward, which put her almost on the table. Stella snorted, earning an irritated glance from the woman. Half-drunk sorority girls showed more restraint and class.

"We need to go," she announced as she reached the table.

Doreen cooed in an unnaturally high voice. "Did you hear that? She's giving orders like she's the boss of you."

Great. She didn't need this. Stella eyed the diner interior. The hunters had left, leaving no one to distract Little Mary Sunshine from what used to be her boyfriend. Now, Stella wasn't too sure, what he was. The man continued to eat, anticipating a catfight over him, no doubt. "I'll wait outside to give the two of you some privacy."

Her eyes stayed fixed on the car outside the glass window. Don't look back, even though her heart shattered a tiny bit with each step across the discolored linoleum floor. Outside, she leaned against the car. To get her mind off the present, she read the various bumper stickers on the nearby car. *Jesus Loves You, but I don't. God, Guns, and Glory make America Great.* Those were the less provocative ones. Many told people what they could do with themselves, their politics, and to get back over the border. Had to be Doreen's car.

Eventually, Cam came out, complaining as he walked toward her. "You didn't have to go and be so nasty."

She waited for the fob beep before wrenching the door open. Once she snapped the seatbelt in place, she felt a little more confident that she'd make it back to the college alive. Cam didn't act anything like the person she thought she knew. Mitch had hinted that Cam's appeal consisted of charm and good looks. Initially, she resisted such inferences. Didn't want to acknowledge what it would say about her. The grumpy Cam climbing into the car was very likely to leave her in the middle of nowhere. Stella would be wandering around in strappy sandals and a maxi dress in the land of chiggers, coyotes, and snakes. An involuntary shudder shook her.

"Are you cold?" Cam turned and looked at her, before

reversing the car. "Looks like you've been crying. No need to, I have no interest in Doreen. Old ugly broad like her could use some charming now and then. I consider it my gift."

Seriously, he thought she was jealous. Even believed she ran to the bathroom for a cry session, incredible. He had more in common with a hollow chocolate bunny than an actual living person. For a smart girl, she'd made a major misstep. Hopefully, it wasn't anything she couldn't correct.

"Quiet, that's a change." Cam turned on the radio but only got static. He punched the CD player button, which filled the car with what Stella referred to as angry rock. A favorite among males, and the occasional female, who felt the world owed them something, but failed to pay up. His taste in music should have served as a hint, but she chose to ignore it, along with dozens of other clues.

They drove back in silence with the soundtrack of screamed lyrics concerning rage, hate, and retribution similar to Doreen's bumper stickers. The two of them would make a great couple. Every couple of miles, he tried to get her to talk. The first time he'd ever wanted her to talk.

The atmosphere in the car weighed heavy, making breathing difficult. It wasn't the air, but more the smugness, the certainty that wafted off Cam. He knew he had her trapped. The thought brought up the half-digested salad into her throat. She gulped the bitter reminder back down. Each moment with him was the equivalent of being stuck with a large hypodermic needle. The storefronts grew familiar as they worked their way through town. Ten blocks from campus, Cam stopped for a red light. She unsnapped her seatbelt, opened the door, yanked her dress to her knees, and jumped out.

"What the hell are you doing?"

She kept walking, not bothering to look back. Traffic tended to be heavy this time of day. Cam would idle through more than one red light. His impatience at having to wait tilted her lips up.

No time like the present to work out issues. If her day went on in the same fashion, Cam would be waiting at her dorm. With that in mind, she veered to her right into a strip mall. The clear glass windows of a Laundromat served as her closest sanctuary. Inside the humid building, she collapsed into a hard plastic chair before calling Leah. Her friend could give her advice about the situation. The phone rang three times before she received a message about the number being out of order. Strange. Her finger hesitated over the three before she tapped it again. Leah was three on her speed dial. She used to be two, but she moved her down when she typed in Cam's number. Should have kept her at two.

Same message. Weird, it made no sense. She'd had the number for three years. Could be there was a phone foul up and would be working in a couple of hours. Mitch would be her next resort. His number was already ringing before she could think of an excuse. She couldn't just ask him if he ever had a DUI. It would sound like she trusted Cam more than she did him.

CHAPTER SEVEN

"HELLO, STELLA. GLAD you called."

Relief and enthusiasm colored Mitch's voice at the same time, making her feel even more the Judas. "Yeah, um, I was wondering if we could talk."

His up tone flat-lined. "Never a good sign. Where are you at?"

Stella glanced at the window, reading the backward lettering. "Henrietta's Wash Tub. It's in the strip mall close to Bacon Street. Do you know where it is?"

"Yeah, I've done my laundry there before. I can be there in ten minutes. Okay?"

"No problem. You don't have to rush." She had no clue what he might be doing. He could be hanging with friends, but more likely studying. Even still, the man would willingly charge to her side, no questions asked. Guilt settled on her along with the damp, fabric-sheet scented air. A girl wearing a college T-shirt folded her laundry out of the dryer. Two small children raced around the row of washers, shrieking despite their mother's entreaties to "settle down." When Mitch came, they'd talk outside without the rumble of dryers or unintended eavesdroppers.

How did one approach this type of thing? Was a DUI considered a criminal record? She didn't know. Specific language in her scholarship forbade any drug or alcohol abuse along with directives that if she did, her scholarship would be revoked.

Mitch came through the door, windblown and breathless as if he'd run the entire way. His dark-rimmed glasses were missing, which gave him a more casual, appealing look. The co-ed folding laundry stopped long enough to smile at him. He didn't even glance at her; headed in Stella's direction.

"Your glasses?" She gestured to the bridge of her nose.

He pulled them out of his pocket and placed them on. "I didn't want them to fall off while I ran."

"Don't you need them to see where you are going?" She tried to imagine Mitch running blindly down the surrounding streets.

"No, just close-up really. That's why I wear them when I'm in the computer lab."

Another thing she didn't know about him. Computer lab and class were the only places she saw him. "Let's walk." She headed in the direction of the doors, glancing over her shoulder to make sure he followed.

Mitch caught up in two long-legged strides and cupped her elbow. "Sure you want to walk in those shoes?" He angled his head at her feet.

"I'm good. As long as you don't walk too fast." The straps on her shoes rubbed against her ankle while her small toe, kept slipping through the toe straps. It stood out like some mutant growth. "I think I'll take them off. It's still warm enough."

Mitch wrapped an arm around her waist as she balanced on one foot and removed her shoes. Once her shoes were off, he dropped his arm, leaving her feeling a bit bereft, but she couldn't ask him to put his arm back, especially when she had to ask personal questions.

"You look very nice for hanging out in a Laundromat."

"Yeah, about that. I got all dressed up because I thought Cam was taking me out on an actual date. Turns out, he was just mad because some of the students were teasing him about seeing you and me together. He drove me way out in the country to a nasty diner that should be in a horror movie."

A menancing growl came from Mitch, but it didn't alarm her. She knew how he felt about Cam. She'd never given his opinion the weight it deserved.

"You know why he drove you to the country, don't you?"

"Because he's a jerk." The memory of her momentary panic at possible abandonment returned.

A long satisfied chuckle answered her response. Happiness flashed in his eyes, crinkling them up at the corners. He cleared his throat. "You're right. He's a jerk in several ways. He chose the out of the way place to minimize anyone thinking you're dating."

She suspected as much, especially after Doreen's comment. There was nothing likable about the place to make someone return. The fact Doreen knew him, meant it was his usual take the naïve chick out on a date hole in the wall location. He probably used the same story about getting back to the date's small town roots. It might have worked a time or two when the girl was from a small town. "Yeah, you're right."

Mitch stopped walking. Stella halted too. He held his hands over his heart while his mouth dropped open. His clownish behavior lightened her mood.

"Stop overacting. You were right all along. Are you happy now?"

Mitch smiled, reached for her hand. "I guess it would be wrong of me to admit that I'm very pleased. Rather petty, small-minded, and all that, but, on the other hand, I don't want to see you unhappy."

"Yeah." Her heavy sigh served as an exclamation point.

"Hey, I'm sorry. I knew you cared about him, but you're better off without him."

His fingers still held onto hers, feeling like a lifeline in a way, but he'd distance himself as soon as she dropped the bomb. Might as well do it now and quit prolonging their false intimacy. "Cam had a lot to say about you."

"The man seems to be obsessed with me. I am no competition for him." Mitch shook his head looking like he couldn't comprehend his rival's actions.

Be brave, spit it out, it will only hurt once, similar to ripping a Band-Aid off. "Cam seems to think you got a DUI in Michigan over the summer."

He dropped her hand just as she suspected he would. His eyes narrowed the same time his hands balled into fists at his side. "Damn it. I thought I got past that."

Well, talk about a revelation. No one appeared to be whom she thought he was. "Do you want to explain? This could ruin your scholarship."

His lifted eyebrows acknowledged the obviousness of her

statement. "I know. It was a stupid thing to do. It was two years ago, not one. Illinois, not Michigan. I was underage too."

"Whoa, that's bad." Her hand covered her mouth before she made any more stupid remarks.

"Yeah." He shoved his hands in his pockets and walked looking down at the ground. "Every month that goes by and I'm that much closer to graduating, I think it won't catch up with me. How did Cam find out?"

Stella shrugged her shoulders. "He didn't say."

Large trees shaded the sidewalk the closer they came to campus. The root system buckled the sidewalk tripping the less alert walker. They both kept their eyes trained on the ground. Stella more to save her toes, but Mitch probably because he saw his future slipping away.

"I was at my cousin's wedding, my favorite cousin, Annalise. She always treated me like a brother she liked, as opposed to the ones she had."

"Go on," she urged. Mitch had never spoken of his cousin.

"It was a big deal wedding. All the stops pulled out. Even had an open bar and a champagne fountain."

No secret how the story would turn out, but there were missing pieces. "You aren't a drinker. When everyone is partying hard, you're at the computer lab working."

"True."

He looked up at her. The misery in his eyes touched her, froze her and caused her to despise Cam more than she ever hated any human being. Mitch continued talking, pulling her from her self-loathing mode.

"I thought I was a big deal too. Annalise asked me to be a

groomsman. I thought I looked like a player in my black tux."
He laughed. "Make that better than usual. I even had a date, a
girl I'd started seeing. We'd been out a few times, and I
thought it might be serious, especially since she accompanied
me to the wedding."

Weddings, unrealistic expectation, and free alcohol, yep
not a good combination. "What happened?" she prompted
when he looked reflective.

"Yeah, that." He cleared his throat again. "Trina must have
heard that weddings were a great place to pick up guys because
she left with a different one."

A swell of anger at the unknown girl's perfidy resulted in
her stomping her foot. "Ow!" Not the best idea when barefoot-
ed.

Mitch immediately bent to examine her foot. "It's not
bleeding." His thumb tenderly brushed the leave debris from
her foot. "Wiggle it." Her toes all flexed, as did her foot. "Not
broken."

Passing students threw them speculative glances. "Get up,
please." By the time, she reached her dorm there would be
gossip that Mitch proposed to her. Not something, she wanted
Cam to hear. It might force him to his next step, which
wouldn't be good.

"So you got drunk because she left you?"

"My intention wasn't to get drunk, but in the end, I guess I
did. My mother had left the reception with her sister. I was
supposed to help break everything down. What I ended up
doing was climbing into my cousin's car, when I shouldn't
have. I promised to drive it back to her house since she left in

the limo."

Stella stole a glance at him. With his shoulders slumped forward, hands in pockets, his chin down, he could have modeled for dejection.

"It's weird the DUI never came out. How long do those things stick on your record?"

"Depends on the state. Usually eight years, sometimes twenty. A deputy who attended the wedding pulled me over. He recognized me. I think I babbled about my date dumping me. Didn't matter, though. I blew over the legal limit. My mother came and picked me up, which was another disappointment in her life. The next morning we picked up the car and drove it to my cousin's house making up some excuse about it being too late the night before. My mother didn't want anyone to know what happened. I figured it would come out then, but never heard anything. Maybe being in a different state had something to do with it. I thought it was behind me. After that, I was super straight, no alcohol, no partying, no weed, nothing."

No partying? Her brows knitted together. "I never took you for an off the chain type."

A rueful smile greeted her remark. "Yeah, with good reason. Bad results. I couldn't afford anything else. The earlier charge could resurrect similar to a zombie with a new one. Still, it puzzles me how Cam Winters would know."

The hum of the riding lawn mower in the distance explained the scent of fresh cut grass. Walnuts littered the sidewalk. Some of the nuts sported a solid green covering, while the majority had black splotches rather like Cam's soul if he had one. Stella's foot intentionally connected with one before, she remembered her bare toes. Sucking her lips in, she kept silent. Complaining about doing a stupid thing would only make her sound like a diva.

Mitch looked at her reddened toes and merely raised an eyebrow. Of course, he had enough on his mind and probably hated her a little right now. Association with her brought him into Cam's manipulative sphere of power, never a good place to be. Her nose crinkled as she remembered her breathless reaction to her initial spotting of the narcissistic man.

Student Life Agency hosted a mixer for the incoming freshmen complete with an inflatable obstacle course and free pizza. Most of the freshmen males showed for the pizza while the upperclassmen concentrated on rating the incoming females. The long shadow of a tree had hidden Stella as she watched Cam work his magic. A ray of sun broke through the clouds serving as a celestial spotlight. At the time, she giggled, thinking even the sun wanted to touch him. Luckily, he hadn't seen her reaction.

Meeting two weeks later, didn't smarten her up. It only made Cam more inaccessible. He'd already burned through all the available hot girls, not even stopping long enough to catch his breath. No wonder she blew him off initially, unable to believe someone like him would be interested in her. Now it seemed his interest came from her work-study position as opposed to her personality. "Do you think Cam went out with me because of my job?"

Mitch lurched, trying to disguise a stumble and eventually stopped. "Are you kidding me?" Both eyebrows rose with his inquiry. "First, you're hot." He held up his index finger. Before continuing, he coughed into his closed fist. "I mean I noticed your personality, your intelligence, your work ethic, but someone like Cam would notice—"

Her friend's politically correct retraction caused her to grin. "Yeah, yeah, I know what you mean. I never knew you thought of me that way." She used her right hand as a fan pretending to be overwhelmed by the notion.

His shoulders went up in a Gallic shrug before turning away. "What good would it have done? I considered myself content in the friend zone."

Students talking loudly about an upcoming concert approached in mass, forcing the two of them off the sidewalk.

"Who knew it was rush hour?" Stella quipped as she walked across the grass. Mitch had liked her, all along. She never knew, while she wasted her time on someone who was only grooming her for future opportunities. Now, thanks to her bad judgment, either she or Mitch would lose their scholarship. She couldn't afford to lose hers, but neither could Mitch.

"I was wondering," Stella started, unsure how to phrase her question. Her hand tucked a lock of hair behind her ear, a tell, Leah would have recognized it immediately. "You've been here longer than I have."

"True." His bent finger pushed up his slipping glasses. He angled his head to the right. "Almost to your dorm."

The aging building indicated she only had a few minutes left. Off to the right, in the side parking lot, a bright spot of red signaled Cam waited. *Oh, joy.* With any luck, she'd escape into the dorm without attracting his notice. Stella darted to Mitch's right side using his silhouette as her safety shield. "Um, you've been here probably as long as Cam has, right?"

"Possibly. I can't say I had that much interest in him. Why do you ask?" Their footsteps mutually slowed as they neared the front door. A female student cradling a clothes basket piled high with clothes gave them a cursory look.

Stella flashed a smile at her, not knowing her name. Instead of responding, the girl rested the basket on one hip as her free hand searched for her ringing cell phone. Glancing back over her shoulder, she measured the girl's progress as she talked. When she thought she was far enough away not to eavesdrop, she asked, "What kind of scholarship is Cam on?"

"What?" Mitch shouted the word and stopped. Stella realizing her Mitch-shaped shield was gone, hurried back to stay in his concealing shadow.

"Lower your voice. I don't want everyone to know." She hissed the words. "Sorry, I don't mean to sound harsh." Conflicting urges to both hide and peek, kept her rooted by Mitch's side, angling just backward enough to glimpse Cam resting against his car with his arms folded and his mouth twisted to one side. She knew the pose, his irritated one. His sunglasses might hide his eyes, but not his body language. A blonde attired only in short shorts and a glorified pushup bra that masqueraded as a top sashayed toward him with enough hip action to merit a future chiropractor visit. Ah Lily, from the third floor, hard not to recognize her. For once, the idea of him flirting with another girl didn't upset her. It gave her the distraction she needed.

"Okay, I asked," she leaned up on her toes, lowering her voice, "if Cam was on any scholarship?"

"Yeah, that's what I thought. Don't see how? An academic scholarship would involve showing up at class. We both know he doesn't do that. If he can't keep up his grades, then a sports scholarship is nil too. Why do you ask?" He pulled off his glasses to polish them on his shirt.

"Cam told me he was going to lose his scholarship because of his grades." The rushed statement sounded ridiculous when she said it. Why did she believe him?

"Hmm," Mitch lengthened the sound, perhaps stalling. "You believed him. Was he trying to work the heartstrings? Maybe you were mad at him?" The corners of his lips tipped up with the inquiry.

"Past mad. He was being a jerk and told me his life would be ruined if his grades didn't miraculously improve," She spat out the words with distaste, realizing how easy he manipulated her emotions. He had her going along with worry for Mitch and concern about him, too.

"What's he expect you to do? Help him with his homework or what?"

Her shoulders went up in *I dunno* shrug. No reason to tell Mitch and have him worry, too. He probably would insist on confessing to DUI. The type of noble, selfless action, she realized Mitch was capable of and Cam wasn't.

"What little I heard from my roommate, who had the bad luck to be Cam's roommate once, is that he comes from money. Already flunked out of one school. With a history like that, not sure why he's trying to pass himself as a scholarship boy. I'm surprised he's lasted as long as he has."

As much as she didn't want it to be true, she realized Mitch's portrait of Cam bore more resemblance to the actual male than her romantic one did. Even when she blessed him with good motives, he was still a selfish man who expected her to help him shop and do laundry. He probably had a harem of other girls doing his academic work. The fact he wasn't passing explained his need to get her to change his grades. They'd been together a couple of months, which made her wonder if she were a backup plan or the original plan all along.

Mitch's hand landed on her shoulder. Her focus moved up to the concern in his eyes.

"Stella, you'd tell me if you were in trouble. If Cam was forcing you to do something you didn't want to."

His words hit so close to home; she had to look away, aware her poker face was nonexistent. "Yeah, yeah, I would." Resting one hand on his arm, she leaned to his left for another peek. Lily's back blocked most of her view of Cam, but the fact Lily and the car remained meant Cam had to be there too. A couple inches of blonde hair showed above Lily's head.

"I need to go now." Rocking to her toes, Stella planted an impulsive kiss on Mitch's cheek. "You're a good friend."

Her fear turbo-boosted her feet, shooting her to the entrance. It didn't stop her from hearing the muttered words. "I wish I knew what was going on."

No, you wouldn't want to know. Her hand pushed open the stairwell door. Adrenalin coursed through her body pushing her up the stairs at a speed any other time would have astounded her. Her fingers pushed into her side trying to push out the muscle spasm. Her hard, raspy breathing echoed in the narrowed stairwell sounding a bit like a B horror movie. The metal banister grew moist under her sweaty hands. A large three loomed on the door ahead of her. Almost there.

A few more steps and she'd be in her room. Sanctuary. Well, of a sort, if her roommate wasn't there. The thought had her sliding down the wall, landing on the cold concrete step. That sucked. Was there no safe place for her?

Sighing deeply, she leaned back against the wall, the railing pushing her head out at an uncomfortable angle. She couldn't stay long in this position. In just a couple of minutes, after she mentally prepped, she'd go. Her roommate would either ignore her as usual or hit her with a barrage of nosey questions. Personally, her regular antisocial behavior would work in Stella's favor.

Her fingers tangled in the full skirt of her sundress she'd donned with high hopes earlier. She'd hoped the malicious skanks would see her with Cam, proving they were an item. Now, Cam disappearing from her life would solve a multitude of problems and improve her mental health in one fell swoop.

Why she ever fell for him puzzled her. Her hand gripped the banister as she pulled herself upright. Leah would listen to her and help her sort things out. After what her best friend had gone through, Cam's machinations would seem like child's play. Falling through time and battling a scorned lover determined to kill her and several others made Stella's situation just college drama.

Leah would help. Maybe she could get Leah's Nana to read her cards via the phone too. If she could get the entire

Carpenter family behind her, then Cam's crazy idea wouldn't happen. The thought calmed her racing heart. It would all work out. She wasn't sure how yet, but it would. Stella took a deep breath, mentally calming herself. When did she talk to her friend last?

A cursory check of the hallway revealed a couple girls walking away from her, giving her a clean shot to her room without talking to anyone. Good. Burnt popcorn stink filled the hallway, crinkling her nose. When she first started school, she called Leah almost every other day. Even though Leah sounded happy whenever she answered, an awkwardness existed between the two of them.

Could be she interrupted her and Dylan? All she did was whine about college while Leah remained upbeat about her experiences. Leah stayed home and went to community college. Not much had changed in her life. No lame room-mates or conniving men who pretended to be her boyfriend. After a while, they didn't talk as much. A couple of times, Leah called when she was with Cam. She hadn't answered, of course.

Her room door swung open, revealing her roommate in the process of leaving. "See you're finally up. You were pixelated last night and never even heard me come into the room."

Stella chose not to correct the assumption certain it would prolong her roommate's departure. "Yeah."

Stepping into the hall, her roommate made space for her to enter the room. Stella had her hand on the door to close it when her roommate spoke.

"The odd couple came by Joe Christian and Wanda Witch wanted me to tell you her cell number changed. She wrote it on the whiteboard."

Stella's roommate had tacked on the unflattering nicknames the first time Dylan and Leah visited. Their insistence on oversized emblems of their faith made it hard not to make wise cracks. Leah now sported a pentacle large enough to set off a metal detector, ironic considering she'd ridiculed the Jesus squad in high school for all their crosses. Then again, her boyfriend was part of the group. In their way, it could be a visual message that faiths could co-exist. Whatever it was, it made people remember them.

The white board near her bed served as her daily to-do list. It also tracked assignments and upcoming tests. Leah's strong emphatic writing brought a sense of normalcy with it. Ignoring her departing roommate, she moved close to the board. Dylan and Leah could still be on campus. If she called now, they might return. That would be glorious. She could do without Dylan, but unlike most males, he knew when to keep his mouth shut or make himself scarce.

Her fingers danced over the phone keypad punching in the numbers. A couple of jabs on the send button resulted in nothing. Why wasn't her phone working? Was it dead? The illuminated battery icon showed almost a full charge. It made no sense. She powered the phone off, and then on, hoping the action would make it work as it did with the computer.

Staring hard at the number, she slowly punched it in again, mouthing each numeral aloud. When she got to the end of the number, a sense of uneasiness assailed her. The last smeared number she thought was a three. It could have been an eight or a five. Next to, it was a tight, cramped memo. *Don't Wreck Yourself Again. Not Sure If I Could Take the Shock. ROTFL*

It had to be her roommate or her slacker boyfriend's writing. A closer inspection revealed the problem. There were only nine digits. Instead of the ten there should have been with the area code. Her idiot roommate erased one accidentally adding her sarcastic note. *Damn it.* She glared at the still open door. There was no Cece in sight.

Stella stomped over to the door and slammed it. The vibration caused her framed poster of the Green Man to tumble from the wall and crack. Despair returned settling on her shoulders, pushing her down to her bed where she curled into a fetal position, dropping her phone by her head. It rang so close to her ear that it practically levitated her off the bed.

Leah. Her hand clutched the phone. Excitement sped up her heartbeat and pushed aside the lethargy that held her down. A glance at the illuminated screen showed Cam's name not her friend's or a new number. Her grip loosened, dropping the phone on the bed. It stopped ringing and then started again. Apparently, Cam would keep it up until she answered.

No other choice. She picked up the phone, powered it off before resuming her fetal position, and pulled the sheet over her head with nowhere she had to be, and nothing she really had to do. Her mind drifted between a consciousness and sleep. A gray, misty land inhabited by bare skeleton trees and whispering voices of people she couldn't see.

CHAPTER EIGHT

S OME OF THE voices became louder and familiar. Her father spat the phrase carved into her heart. "If you hadn't been born, then I would never have stayed with your mother and subjected myself to hell on earth."

A feminine voice, less familiar, but it evoked the combined smells of whiteboard markers, stringent bite of pine cleaning solution, and the mildewed scent she associated with high school gym lockers. "Stella ruined my life."

How did she do that? She couldn't quite remember. The girl's face flickered in and out of focus like a broken video camera. Something about her going out with Jacob whom the girl liked. Jacob something. Nothing ever came of it. She couldn't remember Jacob being that great anyhow.

"I could have won that full ride scholarship if it hadn't been for Stella snatching it away from me. Administrators probably awarded it to her because they felt sorry for her with her crazy ass parents." She recognized the voice of one of her high school classmates, Tricia, an ambitious overachiever whose academic zeal suffered when she started dating the soccer captain.

Did the school administrators feel sorry for her? Did they

promote her as a candidate because her parents insisted on a public airing of their marital troubles? Tricia sounded like she hated her. She thought they were friends, not good friends, but school friends at least. People who saw each other every day and talked about trivial matters. Not the type of friends who called in the middle of the night for a ride.

All she ever did was cause heartache. A coldness settled on her. Her hand searched for the blanket as she kept her eyes tightly closed. No reason to look, she knew what she'd see, the world that had suddenly turned against her. The blanket provided an additional barrier between her and the outside.

Eventually, she found herself back in the land of fog wandering between skeleton trees. Something large hung from a tree, twisting from a rope.

The blurred shape drew her while something inside her urged her to go another way. She knew she should, but her feet kept moving forward as if she'd surrendered all control of her body.

Her heartbeat lunged from its slow, steady space to an all-out run, but her feet didn't comply. She shuffled toward the swinging object. Her body responded as if it belonged to a senior citizen as opposed to someone who hadn't reached her twentieth birthday. Inhaling deeply, she drew on her meditative practice to slow her heart and ease her building anxiety. It didn't help.

Her inability to draw a deep breath left her panting like a dog. As she drew closer to the tree, the shape faded, and then sharpened, startling her with the image of a hanged man. The wind tussled with the body, gradually turning it. Stella recog-

nized the long, lanky body and the dark hair before the final twist of the rope revealed the face. The skin above the tight noose swelled due to the restricted blood flow, turning a bruised reddish purple.

The scream never came. Unable to push it past her panting, it lodged in her throat, making the simple act of taking in oxygen even more problematic. The grotesque image of her friend hanging held her gaze. His eyes opened, causing her to stumble back a few steps, tripping over a tree root and landing on her butt. Her hands took the brunt of her fall. Her attention stayed on Mitch's head. His lips moved.

"Stella, you did this!"

Her hand flew up to her chest, holding in a heart that threatened to beat out of her chest. "How did I do this? I care about you. I never want anything bad to happen to you."

"Care! Does this look like the act of a concerned friend? You had the ability to stop Cam, but you chose not to. The only person you care about is yourself."

Oh, she had contemplated doing nothing; certain Cam's threats were meaningless. Who knew it'd come to this. "I don't understand. Cam only threatened your scholarship."

"My scholarship, my reputation, my credibility, my only chance to get ahead. Sure, I've done things I've regretted. It looked like I would finally triumph over them until you came along disturbing everything I'd built with your desire to have every guy at your feet."

"It wasn't like that." How could she make him understand? His eyes closed, and the wind twisted the rope, turning him *away from her.*

Stella woke with a jerk. Sweat drenched her tired body. Her muscles burned reminding her of her earlier attempts to take up running. After what her runner acquaintances called a light jog, she'd be nauseous, dizzy, and shaking, like now.

What happened to her? Bad dream, for sure, but it shouldn't drain her. What if it wasn't a dream, but was a glimpse of the future? It would mean her father was right. She destroyed everything and everyone she touched. What if she caused Mitch's suicide?

There didn't seem to be any way out of her dilemma. It would help to talk to Leah. Lately, she'd been such a bad friend, not returning her calls until Leah might think she no longer cared about their friendship, especially when she didn't call after she'd left her new number. In the end, it was hard to know who could help her. Possibly her mother? A deep breath escaped her. College served as a buffer between her and her mother. Still, mothers were supposed to help, part of their job description or something.

An inner voice, she'd called intuition and her spirit guide, urged her not to call her mother. "I have to. There's no one else. Besides, moms are supposed to love you when no one else does. You can always go home when things are bad."

A brief memory of one of her fellow students dropping out of school when her ultra-conservative parents stopped paying tuition after she came out. "That's her parents, not mine. My mom will be there for me, even if my father isn't." Stella lowered her voice, well aware of the ridicule her talking to herself would inspire.

Steeling herself, she readied herself for the call. Her mother never qualified as the warm and fuzzy type. When she fell and bloodied her knee as a toddler, her mother would wipe it with a burning antiseptic and put a bandage on it. No kissing it and making it better or rocking her until the tears stopped. Practical, that's what her mother was. The woman made lists, followed plans, and got things done. Well, she used to until her dad walked out.

The phone in her hand, she scrolled down to home listing. Her mother passed her organizational skills to her, which allowed her to rise to the top of her class and snag the coveted scholarship. Sucking in her lips, she tried to still the voices that warned her not to call. Seriously, what could happen? If her mother gave her bad advice, she didn't have to act on it. No reason to tell her everything.

Her thumb hit the call button, ending the dilemma. The familiar sound of her mother's voice brought reassurance. She seemed friendly, normal, not like the frenzied woman yelling at her fleeing spouse, nor did she sound like the woman constantly quoting paraphrased Bible verses. True, Stella would never qualify as a Biblical scholar, but she did know the line, God helps those who help themselves, came from *The Grapes of Wrath*, not the Bible.

"Hi, Mom. It's me, Stella."

Her mother chuckled. The sound brought with it a surge of warmth. When was the last time she heard her mother laugh?

"What's so funny? Would you like to share with the class?" she teased her mother already feeling better about calling.

Dropping the blanket, she sat up, straightening her spine, her mother's mantra coming automatically to mind. Good posture made every woman look good. It not only made a female's figure look better, but also conveyed confidence.

"You, thinking I wouldn't recognize your voice or the cell number I pay for every month with the pittance I receive from your father. That's the good months when he pays on time and isn't plane hopping with his Jezebel of a wife to the various fleshpots like Vegas and Paris." Her voice became shriller, losing any warmth as she spoke.

Stella moved the phone from her ear, not needing it close to hear, as her mother grew progressively louder. She didn't call to talk about her father. His desertion and young new wife had been discussed to death in her opinion. Jezebel and fleshpots must mean she was still attending psychos-be-us church. Paris a fleshpot? Never thought of it that way.

"Mom, let's not talk about Dad. I have a problem that I wanted to run past you." Even as she said the words, she had doubts. It would be great if someone could be a neutral sounding, board. The practical mother she used to know could come up with a logical solution. Although, her mother's current way of solving problems involved allowing a Bible to fall randomly open and poking at a verse with her eyes closed, would not help her.

"Don't tell me, you're pregnant, you little slut!" The snarled words sounding like an alcohol-fueled rant. No wonder, she'd been so friendly at first enjoying a warmth that came from too many Long Island Teas.

"No!" Her answer came automatic, equally angry that her

mother would call her a slut. Why did she call? All she wanted to do was hang up. Of course, she couldn't just hang up. That would be rude as if calling her a slut wasn't harsh. "Never mind now doesn't seem like a good time."

"Good time? Whadya mean a good time. There's never a good time. We're all going to die. Are you ready to die?"

Stella placed the phone on the bed as she shot both hands into her hair, cradling her head. Her mother's question echoed in her head. Was she ready to die? She could hear her mother still talking about ending up in a lake of fire. Ready to die, it would be like going to sleep if she did it right. A long restful sleep where she'd never have to worry about Cam or Mitch accusing her of ruining his life. Without her to threaten, Cam would have no leverage and wouldn't go through with his plans since no one could execute them.

The idea took root, calming her. She picked up the phone, ready to hang up, knowing she didn't have to worry about offending her mother if she were no longer around.

"Stella, you're not still part of that witchy nonsense. That's your problem. You need to get into a real church. I'll get Pastor Jim to recommend a few places near the campus."

Not caring about the furor her words would cause or maybe wanting to needle her, she said, "Oh yes, still involved. In fact, I'm head high priestess now. Every full moon, we strip naked, hop on our broomsticks and fly. Only after, we down a couple goblets of innocent babies' blood. We can buzz your house if you'd like."

Her terminating the call cut her mother's anguish cry of, "No!" short.

A stillness surrounded her as she contemplated her room. On her side, color-coded storage boxes stood in straight towers with neat labels. Clipboards with various lists hung from nails. Her need to control her environment took organizational to a completely new level. Apparently, it hadn't worked.

The open dresser drawers, wrecked closet, and the pile of odiferous clothing crowded her roommate's side proving that organization didn't always win the day. Cece, the name her roommate insisted on—despite the room assignment list declared it was Charlotte—for the most part, acted happy. If Stella discounted the times Cece was high, asleep, or out and out snarky, then she was happy. Probably happy then too, especially when acting like a total jerk. Cece's slacker boyfriend suited her too. Picking a boyfriend out of her league never worked, not that she had all that much experience, but she did now.

Pills. She needed pills. Maybe Cece had something she could take. Stella pawed through the open drawer, moving around half-eaten cookies, crushed crackers, wadded paper, thongs, unmatched socks, and a container of birth control pills. She held up the plastic container. "Nope, the best it would do would probably cause water gain if I took the whole package. You'd think she'd have something. Then again, the girl was all about getting high, not dying."

People died all the time from mixing drugs, often prescriptions, and alcohol. Being underage never served as an obstacle to getting drunk. Plenty of drugs on campus, too, but she didn't know any dealers. Asking around would cause some raised eyebrows and with her luck, a call home. Prescription drugs would be her best bet. She'd heard the nurse practitioner at the campus clinic wrote out prescriptions without even blinking an eye, especially on the weekends. Most of the students faked their injuries for a pain killer or muscle relaxer. She'd overheard two students talking about it while working in the computer lab. Enough pills created a floaty high, very relaxing. It made sense that taking all the pills with a fifth should do the trick.

Injury, what type should she have? An outward one wouldn't work since a lack of physical symptoms would be easy enough to disprove. *Focus.* The word reminded her of her father who often chanted the word to hone her critical thinking skills. "Yeah, thanks a lot, Dad." Her bitter words hung in the air.

Maybe she should compose a heartstrings-pulling suicidal note. No. Everyone had to think it was an accident, especially Cam. Still, she could look good. Do her best to have good posture as she stretched out in bed, which would please her mother. The absurdity made her giggle. Of course, she'd be on to her next life, hopefully, a better one. Wasn't real clear on that aspect. With any luck, she might get a choice. Who knows she could come back as an animal, hopefully, a well-loved pet.

There had to be something she could use to get drugs. The idea of looking it up on the Internet beckoned, but someone could check her history. Mitch would still be able to trace her cyber footsteps even if she erased them. Knowing him, he'd blame himself. Definitely, didn't want that for the only truly decent male she'd ever met. Sure, Leah's brother, Ethan was okay too. Even Dylan, Leah's boyfriend, managed a spot on the decent male list, but Mitch held the only romantic possibilities. Not that much would come of it, now. If he'd discovered what a mess she'd made he'd never speak to her. At least dead, he'd think positive thoughts of her. After a while, she'd be a faded memory, some girl he knew in college who overdosed on muscle relaxers. Yeah, muscle relaxers would work.

The scent of cinnamon drifted on the air as she opened the exterior door. The spice had her imagining students clutching mugs of hot apple cider as they chatted. Could be someone got ambitious and used the communal kitchen. More likely, the nutrition centers, as the school liked to call the cafeterias, were trying out some seasonal favorites. The thought of stopping in to see what it was tempted her.

Don't go there. You have a mission. Killing herself didn't seem like a quest, but everyone would be better off. Mitch wouldn't lose his scholarship. Her mother would get the insurance money, and with any luck, she wouldn't give it to her 'you'll die a fiery death' church. Her father could no longer blame her for ruining his life.

A huge maple tree with the scarlet leaves served as her landmark for the clinic. The modern concrete building did not fit in with the stately brick academic buildings. Adding a clinic for students' medical and mental needs had to have been an afterthought. Apparently, earlier students were healthier or toughed it out. No cars in the front parking lot and only an older sedan in the side lot. A dent marred the car in the side parking lot.

Car wreck, yeah that would work for a cover story. Constant pain from the car wreck last year. What hurt? People were always complaining about something hurting. Her back, yeah, that was good since back pain hurt no matter if you were standing, sitting, or even lying down. Couldn't question it either, since it was a matter of perception.

A male student staffed the front desk. He glanced up and immediately closed the computer screen with a blush, assuring Stella it wasn't anything academic. "Can I help you?"

"Yes, I'd like to see whoever is on duty about pain." She pressed her hand to her lower back and grimaced. "Back pain."

"Okay." He pushed forward a clipboard. "Sign in. Your medical card is on file?"

Medical card. Didn't even consider that. Hadn't come to the clinic before. "Yes." Her answer satisfied him since he only glanced at her name before vanishing behind the file cabinets. He returned in under a minute.

"You can go in." He gestured to a door behind him, not even bothering to look up.

Stella slowly walked in, realizing her choice would be a permanent solution to a temporary issue. At least that is what all the suicide prevention stickers had printed on them. Still, it wasn't a simple matter of being embarrassed because she sexted the wrong person. As for her life, it hadn't been good for a while. When was life a joy as opposed to some daily obstacle course she ran, hoping not to screw up too much? Somewhere in high school, back when she and Leah were a team, before Dylan.

A middle-aged woman with frizzy hair and reading glasses perched on her nose looked up from her computer. "What brings you here?" The tired tone of her voice announced her disinterest.

"Pain." She touched her back and repeated her grimace while wondering if she could fool a medical professional as well as she did the student out front. The white lab coat intimidated Stella, convincing her she could see through her hasty fabrication.

"Cramps?" The woman raised an eyebrow. The unspoken message conveyed that she had no sympathy for crybaby students who showed up with female complaints.

"No, oh no, ma'am. I wouldn't come to a clinic because it was my time of the month." She watched the woman's face shift from disdain to possible caring. Difficult to measure, but the ma'am helped.

"This pain, what causes it?" She gestured for her to continue, as she typed something on her computer.

Stella stretched her neck seeing her name on a file. She wondered if her parents would obtain the file with her false accident on it. Even if they did, it would be too late to do anything about it. "Car accident."

"Recently? Were you a passenger or a driver?" She swiveled and typed a few more words.

Car accident. Would there be a record for that? Would it have done enough damage to get painkillers? "I was hit by a car." The woman's gaze snapped back to hers.

"On campus?"

The inquiry brought back the belief that campus accidents guaranteed free tuition if you were the pedestrian, not the driver. Stella considered it an urban myth, but maybe it wasn't.

Plenty of students probably claimed accidents hoping for a free ride. "Oh no, it was back in my hometown. Messed up my bike, totaled it. Did a number on my hip and spine. Put me in traction."

The woman clicked her tongue and shook her head, muttering something about a helmet or lack of one. Stella considered pointing out that a helmet would not have helped her spine or hip but didn't. Instead, she waited silently for the nurse's summation.

"You look fine now."

Seriously, her makeup smudged from crying made her look somewhat ragged. "I'm not. Constant pain with the weather change. Causes my back to act up." She pushed out a whimper that sounded far from convincing.

"Hmm. It's a gorgeous fall day." A disdainful look settled on the nurse's face.

Who said this woman gave out pills similar to candy? Stella staggered to the wall, putting a hand on it. "It hurts to stand. It hurts to sit, too." She used the same complaints her former neighbor used after breaking several bones when rear-ended by a semi. The woman always sported a visible pain patch. She needed pills, not a patch.

After an exam, in which Stella manage to moan, grimace and shudder, she received two foil wrapped sample packs of painkillers and muscle relaxers. Pocketing the proffered pills, she wondered if they'd be enough.

The practitioner wrote something down on a prescription pad then tore it off and handed it to Stella. It could be a prescription for more painkillers, which would mean she'd have to find a way to the pharmacy.

"This is an order for X-rays at the local hospital. Get this done as soon as possible and have them sent here. Dr. Lomax will want to look at them before prescribing any medicine. If you take one pill every eight hours, it's enough to make it through the weekend."

Enough to make it through the weekend. Not enough. "I will, ma'am. There's no chance of overdosing, is there?"

"Good question. Not too many students would be conscientious enough to ask. No problem as long as you don't take them all at once." She gave a slight chuckle. "I can tell you're not the type."

Stella nodded, keeping her face expressionless. Samples in one hand and X-ray order in the other, she exited the building. Cece usually spent the weekend with her boyfriend, which would save her from any efforts to rescue her. She'd pull up the covers over her head just in case. That way, Cece would leave her alone, thinking she was asleep.

Decision made she kept her gaze forward. Anything could distract her from her intention from a squirrel gathering food for the upcoming winter to the outstretched branches of the Pin Oak tree that marked the entrance to the library where a male walked down the steps. A peripheral vision caught the familiar figure striding down the stairs. Mitch. She'd probably interrupted his studies when she called him from the Laundromat.

If only he'd come over and tell her how much he needed her, she'd forget the plan. Her fingers tightened around the sample packages. The sharp foil-wrapped cardboard bit into her palm. Her eyes fixed on a sign about the upcoming billiards and beard contest. She came to college for this. The total of the educational experience included growing facial hair and hitting balls with a stick. There'd be beer, too, but that didn't merit a mention since it was a staple of college life.

Mitch continued down the stairs, staring at an open book in his hands. Her feet carried her away from an accidental meeting. Just as well, since her intention would result in a better life for the one person who actually cared about her. Weren't you supposed to sacrifice for those you cared about? If she used her father as an example, there came a time you quit sacrificing and did whatever you wanted.

Her stride quickened as she neared her dorm. Cece could never be counted on being predictable, which meant Stella needed to be dead by the time she returned when she wasn't too sure, how long it would be. None of those news reports gave details. The incredibly brief reports summed up one person's struggle with life and his eventual defeat in two sentences. Edward Norwood, forty-one, found dead in home, drug overdose suspected, with nothing about Edward's love of silent movies or his collection of model trains. Not a single line about how he bought dozens of Girl Scout cookies every year and gave them away. Not a word about Edward falling deeply in love when he was twenty-two, only to have the woman reject him. Excluded were the details that Edward hated his job and his boss was a jerk. Factors such as being behind on his rent and possible eviction never appeared in the paper. Stella shook her head slowly. No wonder the man committed suicide even if he was only a figment of her imagination.

A dark haired girl approached with a smile and waved. Stella half-smiled. Unsure if she should put up her hand clutching the pills. Odd, on her last day of life, that someone would be friendly, especially since she found the females on the campus to be singularly unfriendly. Too much, like high school where you were either competition or a wing-woman. Competition in regards to grades, dates, or even popularity turned women against one another. No one had anything to worry about from her. While her grades weren't bad, they weren't stellar curve setting ones from high school.

As for being a wing woman, she didn't know enough viable males to serve as an introduction. The wing woman traditionally needed to be less attractive than the woman who was trying to hook the man. Mitch considered her very beautiful. His declaration baffled her since she saw the same face in the mirror every day of her life. It had changed over the years. Her plump cheeks thinned down into smooth curves while her teeth straightened thanks to braces. Not sure if she'd ever consider herself beautiful, but enough of the female populace saw her as a threat. The part, who didn't, because they were too involved with their boyfriend or school, didn't have a need for her friendship. Why kid herself, she wasn't known for her upbeat banter or perky attitude. Leah had served as her only real friend in high school.

The scholarship dictated her school choice, not friends or lack of friends. It didn't matter at first because of so much activity that first couple of weeks. Some girls even tried to befriend her until they realized she wasn't the party type and only came to school for an education. Maybe the dark haired girl was one of them. Her wave could be her second stab at friendship. Could be she needed Stella somehow. How could she desert her potential friend?

As the female drew closer, Stella's smile grew wide as she racked her brain for a name without success. Instead of meeting her eyes, the woman drifted by yelling a greeting once she passed. Twisting backward, Stella saw her potential friend, who was going to need her in some fashion to delay her suicide, talking to another girl. Whatever. Why did she expect a friend when she hadn't had one the three months she'd been here?

Better to check out now before things got ugly. People checked out all the time in different ways. Her father chose divorce, which left an ugly scar behind. Her mother in one of her many rants about him mentioned death would have been kinder because she would have gotten both sympathy and insurance benefits.

Her hand landed on the exterior door. The first tug didn't budge it. Strange since it remained unlocked during the day. A second firm tug pulled it open and sent her staggering back a step. An errant wind blew across the campus, creating tiny funnels of fallen leaves and slammed the door she'd just opened.

Odd. That wind coming out of nowhere. Her third attempt opening the door produced nothing. Could be the lock tripped with the slam. Talk about a sucky day. Couldn't even get into the building successfully. Never mind the conscientious nurse practitioner who wouldn't give her a full bottle of pills. Her feet landed on the leaves with a satisfying crunch as she stomped around the building to the front rotating door.

The freshmen buildings still had the archaic spinning doors. Supposedly, it helped keep the lobby heated. The simple concept baffled drunk or high students as they walked in an endless circle never getting anywhere. Stella had chuckled when she'd witnessed a trio of smashed girls spinning around but never getting into the lobby. Their dizzying journey stopped when the muscular catcher for the softball team stepped in behind them.

The infamous door was empty. Success. She sprinted for it to get in before some joker came in behind her at a run, enjoying the prospect of a prank that'd send her around for a couple of loops. She stepped into the lobby after only a half turn. Orange and brown couches faced each other in conversational settings. Could be the colors reflected someone's idea of warmth for students far away from everything they held familiar. More likely, the furniture came from a faculty area remodeling. Freshmen always got the rejects. Administration and professors didn't have much investment in freshmen because so many never returned. The praise, awards, and new furniture went to juniors and seniors who enriched the school with their continuous tuition payments.

Her feet slowed as she walked to the elevator. She could take the steps but abandoned the idea, picturing herself stuck in some stairwell, unwilling to make the last few steps to her floor. The elevator door pinged open. Two girls both on their cell phones sauntered out without acknowledging Stella. Not too surprising since she doubted they even glanced at one another.

On the elevator, she punched her floor button while considering all the symbols she'd passed. The leaves falling off the tree indicated a circle of life. Not everyone lived to be eighty-three. Most didn't. The rotating door made her wonder if she'd spent her entire life walking in a circle. Everyone who walked past her without a smile, a word, or recognition that she existed signified she might as well not be there. Then there were the people that her presence merely irritated from the rude waitress at the diner to the student worker she'd surprised at the clinic. She could probably live her life out with no recognition and the occasional jerk.

She couldn't destroy life for Mitch the way she had for her father. The elevator jerked a little. Her hand gripped the railing wrapped around the inside of the car. It reminded her why she preferred the stairs. The unit must be on its final cycle, too. The cable could snap, hurling her to the basement, ending her dilemma. The thought made her lips tip up slightly.

The fact the building contained only four stories meant, she'd only break something and be in pain. Not good, not something she wanted. When the doors swooshed open, she breathed a sigh of relief. Music blared from several rooms in an undeclared war of musical genres. Normally, she did her best to ignore it as she walked to her room. Today, she listened. A happy reggae beat greeted her. The inhabitant could be from Jamaica or simply embraced a Jamaican outlook. Two more strides carried her into the sounds of an angry woman wailing about the injustice of life. *Yeah, understand where the singer is coming from. The real question was why did the woman keep trying?*

The sound of strings and woodwinds had Stella stopping. The number on the door read fourteen. No name card under it meant someone who didn't want anyone knocking on her door and introducing herself or, worse yet, wanting to borrow something. Borrow translated into you'll never see this item again, except on a post in social media with the borrower wearing it. Yeah, whoever was in room 14 may have been worth knowing. Something inside her opened up with a longing for a possible friend behind the undecorated door. If she stared at it long enough, it might swing open, revealing the missing cog in her support network. Stella turned; realizing her mental grabbing at straws only delayed the inevitable with no reason to stay and every reason to go.

Inside her empty room, the stink of Cece's unwashed clothes hung in the air, mingling with something dead, a mouse in the wall most likely. The janitor staff put out poison never making the connection that the rodents would not conveniently exit the building before breathing their last. Her nose crinkled, but she wouldn't have much longer to endure it anyhow. *Did people smell on the other side? If they did, what did they smell?*

A quick search of her roommate's side of the room netted her a half of bottle of vodka. It'd do. Her arm cleared her nightstand, brushing the lamp, radio clock, and her daily planner to the floor. She placed the bottle of vodka on the stand along with the muscle relaxers and pain pills. The pills she lined up similar to waiting floats in a parade. She popped the first pill in her mouth and took a large swig of liquor. The harsh burn of the liquid nearly had her spitting out the pill in reaction, but she held on. The room appeared the same, nothing changed. *Yeah, one pill wasn't going to do it.*

Three pills sat in her cupped hand. She forgot which color was a painkiller, but it didn't matter. She carefully placed the pills on her tongue before taking another swallow of the cheap liquor. College students favored the brand because of its potency and price. *This is horrible for my liver.* The random thought made her wonder briefly if any of her body could be organ donation quality. When she received her driver's license, she'd agreed to be an organ donor. Someone might as well make use of her body since she wouldn't be using it.

The thought made it easier to swallow the last four pills. A lethargy slid over her, relaxing her muscles, fogging her mind. Her hand wrapped around the bottleneck. Holding it up to eye level, it looked as if two cups remained. Cups were not the proper term her mind insisted. Must drink it all. Can't take chances. The liquor spilled out of the side of her mouth. Was her throat even swallowing? The tinkling of the bottle hitting the floor came from a distance as a fast moving fog obscured everything.

CHAPTER NINE

W AS SHE ASLEEP, lying down, or even dead? *She never got around to cleaning up. Dead people never thought about makeup, did they?* A sensation of movement lifted her up. Underneath the fog, she could see silhouettes of buildings, occasionally something moving that could be a car. Was it moving or was she? If so, was she flying? Would her arms be stretched straight out like plane wings the way she played as a kindergartener? The thought amused, making her want to mimic her younger behavior.

Her arms didn't work. *Weird.* Wiggle fingers. Nothing. Stella glanced down at her body, seeing more clouds drifting by as opposed to her body. *Was this death? Did she suddenly vanish when her heart stopped?*

She swallowed the ball, which had formed in her throat. *Did she swallow? Did she even have a throat? Dead was so much more confusing than she thought it would be. Where was Summerlands, Heaven, or Hell?*

A beige fog surrounded everything. Her mother's voice spoke, "This way."

Stella drifted closer to the source. Odd, her mother, could arrive so fast after her death, but maybe time moved slower on this side. The shadows of people moving like dark ants under the cloud cover attached to her mother's voice.

"We have to be quick before anyone sees us."

The rising hysteria had become practically second nature to her mother as her marriage worsened and finally ended. It was another reason why Stella applied to colleges that weren't a commutable distance.

Her spirit hovered over the four people scurrying across the campus. The clouds shifted revealing her mother, the shifty con artist minister, and two muscle-bound men who could have doubled as biker bar bouncers. Their appearance confused her. Wasn't sure why the minister came unless it was another attempt to save her soul. *Wonder how much mom paid for this house call. Make that dorm call. Salvation visit?*

"This door." Her mother opened the back door Stella had so much trouble opening earlier.

Hovering above them, Stella watched the group snake up the stairs. Her mother led the group acting as a spy leading a mission.

Was this what dead would be like, constantly watching the living? It didn't sound like much fun. Her mother's behavior intrigued her. Would she freak out when she found her dead body?

They were at her door. Instead of knocking, her mother opened the door, demonstrating she'd never locked it. "Whoa, smells like something died in here."

Mr. Sleazy Minister grabbed her mother's arm. "Wait! Demons are inside. I must cast protection first." The man withdrew a vial from an inside pocket and shook it side to side.

"Begone evil spirits. By the power invested in me, I cast you out." The man shook, then put out his hands and grappled with something.

Nothing. You think being dead would give me supernatural vision, and I could see the demons.

He pocketed the vial and turned to the waiting three. "It's safe. I see the possessed collapsed on her bier of filth."

Harsh, it would make sense if he were referring to Cece's bed, but I wash my sheets every week.

One of the bruiser guys stepped into the room and looked in the direction the minister pointed. "Passed out if you ask me."

The response earned a glare from the minister who mouthed the word, *possessed.*

"Yeah, yeah. That's what I meant. Possessed and passed outlook so much alike.

The body interests me, considering it was my body. The bouncer first in the room knelt and picked my body up gently. I didn't feel anything, but I guess the dead never do. My arms flopped down, and my head lolled obscenely to the side. My mouth gaped open. What a mess!

The men left the room with the minister in the lead, holding a wooden cross in front of him. Did he think B-movie vampire girls inhabited the dorm? Of course, as movie vampires they'd wear revealing outfits or lingerie. If a student did pop out of her room, she'd be sporting a T-shirt, yoga pants, and no vampire fangs.

The muscle men's heads swiveled side-to-side checking the area around them as they moved silently down the hall. Her mother trailed behind, biting her lips and looking slightly dazed as if she were the one who'd taken a handful of pills and washed them down with alcohol.

If she were dead, her mother's behavior would be understandable.

Dead? She didn't feel anything. What about the white light and her dead relatives welcoming her to the great beyond. A glance down the hallway revealed a red exit sign. Somewhat appropriate, but not the light at the end of the tunnel. No relatives were in sight, except her mother, who was still alive.

What was the deal? Shouldn't they notify the administration? Call an ambulance. One man climbed into the back of the dark SUV, and then the other one passed her body inside. Her mother opened the front passenger door without a tear on her face. Her earlier confusion gave way to her trademark expression, a pursed mouth reflecting a rotten flavor on her tongue. It indicated things were not going her way.

Yeah, daughter committing suicide would do that to her. Not something to brag about. As the only child, Stella bore the brunt of carrying the family banner. Only children had to meet all the parents' dreams and expectations since no spare existed. She'd dropped it in the mud this time. No possibility of redemption either.

Leah's grandmother, Esmeralda Hare, would shrug her shoulders and say, "It is what it is."

None of that easy acceptance of events that fate dealt them for her family. Nope. Her family raged at the injustices, the tears in the life plan. Everything was personal, deliberate, and malicious. No doubt, her father would view her death as a way to cast a cloud on his happiness with his new wife, Bunny or Barbie. Couldn't remember her name since her mother usually made up a different one every time she ranted about her. She probably thinks the names are insulting as opposed to lame.

The black SUV got smaller as she went higher. The tree branches studded with a few remaining leaves made it hard to see the ground, but not impossible. The four-lane road that cut through the campus contained a black SUV. It could be them, her. Hard to think of the slack body as hers. How could it be when she was in the clouds similar to a passenger in an airborne plane?

The buildings, sidewalks, and roads resembled a topographical map. It reminded her of the one she made in fifth grade, except there was no oatmeal box-shaped cylinder buildings. There weren't any in her town either, but due to limited box supply, she'd improvised. Yeah, her family majored in improvising. Only once they improvised, they pretended it was always what they wanted, even planned for, until it wasn't. A watery shine drew her eye.

The local lake shimmered underneath her. The term lake gave the body of water more grandeur than it merited. A lifeguard stand and a thin strip of beach marked one end of the water. Originally, the park served as a community park that failed. A thick chain link fence encompassed the water for safety. Difficult to see from this high up, but she knew it was there. It wasn't enough to keep out drunk college students intent on an evening of skinny-dipping. More than one person drowned in the endeavor. Would their ghosts be hanging out there by the water's edge?

A small strip of something white fluttered in the breeze. Her narrowed eyes couldn't bring it into focus. Not a ghost or at least nothing resembling the transparent figures often seen in movies. Spirits usually chose invisibility, according to Leah's grandfather. People tended to freak out, which didn't mean ghosts weren't there. Obviously, no one noticed her hovering in the sky similar to a parade balloon.

The landmarks grew smaller until only splotches of color. Green over here indicated the forest. A spattering of dark dots meant houses. A winding strip of silver could be either the river or a highway. Clouds blocked her vision as she ascended to who knows where. The concept of heaven was one she denied years ago, especially the one populated with angels strumming harps. It made no more sense that angels perched on clouds, than fiery demons existed below the ground. If that were the case, wouldn't an astronaut catch a glimpse of a celestial city as he hurtled through space?

Of course, it didn't stop it from existing even if she didn't believe in it. Her knowledge of the afterlife consisted of her mother warning her she'd burn in hell if she didn't change her ways. Would she meet a Biblical saint in white robes, who'd question her life? It could be that some grand entity didn't resemble humans at all. What if there were huge dog statues outside the gates? That would be nice. A world ruled by canines. There would be plenty of trees, endless fields, and the occasional cat.

Her drifting upward stopped with a bump. Had she reached the edge of the atmosphere? She put up her hands to feel but encountered no obvious barriers. She felt nothing. Did her fingers actually work? She held up one hand but saw nothing but a gray vapor. Was she disappearing? An unfamiliar voice sounded to her left.

"I think we should tie her up."

Whom were they tying up?

Her mother's voice added, "Do you have to? It seems like overkill, especially since she's unconscious." A hint of entreaty colored the request. Completely different from the way her mother made any request sound as if issuing a royal edict. Do this or be banned from the kingdom. To be fair, her mother's opinion usually proved right. Well, right about practical things. That was before the foundation of her world cracked. She didn't recognize the uncertain woman who sounded like her mother, but acted more like a victim.

"Don't be fooled, sister. The demons that possess her know many tricks. Tying her is a necessity. We'll also need to sprinkle her with holy water."

In the one brief conversation Stella had with her father since the separation, he'd asked if her mother were still seeing the strange minister. She'd assume he meant church attendance, not an actual relationship. Besides, calling someone sister wasn't too romantic. What was the deal with the water anyhow? As far as she knew, only Catholics felt the need to bless the water. Water as one of the four elements was naturally sacred.

Her mother's voice regained vigor as she argued. "I know we need to rid her of the demons, but a hospital would serve too, much better than this filthy shack."

"Sister, you forget yourself. Even being close to your diseased child has infected you. Perhaps we need to start the exorcism with you."

Exorcism. Whoa, she didn't want that! The ominous words hung in the air. Leah had told her about some church that performed exorcisms and killed people in the process. Their rationale was at least they saved the person from eternal damnation, if not death. Somehow, she needed to explain she wasn't possessed. Wait. Would it matter if she were already dead?

In fact, why was she still here? Didn't spirits move on to wherever they had to go unless their death was unexpected? Hers wasn't. Her preoccupation with the present and the transportation of her body must have prevented her from leaving. Somehow, she needed to move on to whatever the next realm was.

The sound of the arguing became softer as a beige fog revealed the skeleton tree forest. She'd been here before. This was it, huh. Her feet moved soundlessly toward the mist covering them each time they encountered the soft ground. She assumed it was dirt because of the trees. No moon or sun hung in the cloudy sky, but a weak light illuminated the scenery from behind, throwing shadows everywhere.

If this were the passage to the other world, where were the welcoming relatives? C'mon now, she had some. Grandma Laney and Grandpa Jim both died in a car accident when she was ten. Her grandparents' death turned her spontaneous mother into a control freak, someone who had to have everything planned. Her Aunt Gigi should be here too. Gigi, her mother's only sister, used to spoil Stella the way indulgent single aunts did with gifts from her various travels as an international flight attendant. She even brought the kimono Gigi gave her to college. A brain aneurysm took the vibrant, confident woman right before Stella's birthday. Her mother blamed third world health care because it happened when she was overseas.

No Aunt Gigi motioned her forward with a grin. No Grandpa Jim patting his pocket where he hid a supply of her favorite soft peppermint candy. No Grandma Laney held her arms wide open. No one. Loneliness swamped her, causing her to stumble, almost falling into the mist. Her hands caught on her knees before she face planted into the fog. If she tumbled into the mist, it would be the end. The thought had no basis as it popped into her head.

Only trees without a leaf or bud to mark the season dotted the landscape. Not that unusual, if they were dead. It felt like strolling through a botanical graveyard. A chill had her chafing her arms and peering into the shadows. No wonder her mother went all controlling since her relatives disappeared in a span of three years, leaving only her husband and Stella. It explained the obnoxious behavior of nosing into every aspect of Stella and her father's life. Her lips tightened as she considered the possibility that her father could have already cheated. Life sucked.

Death, however, was no picnic, either. Where was every-one? She couldn't be the only person who died today. Did each person rate a personal hell or purgatory? "Am I all alone here?" The words echoed through the trees mocking her. An echo indicated they bounced off a hard surface, possibly rock or even a ravine captured her words and threw them back to her.

Great. A huge gaping hole existed somewhere. She'd probably stumble into it and break her neck. The ground-hugging fog would make such an accident a certainty. Panic welled up inside her, making her want to break into a run. Logic prevailed. "I'm dead. What else can happen?"

The sound of something swaying drew her. The first sound she'd heard in this silent tomb of a place. Off to her left, a creaking rode the wind. It reminded her of the swing on Grandmother Laney's porch. A twinge ran across her shoulders.

"Someone walked over my grave," she murmured the words. Although not cheery, it helped hearing a human voice, even if it was hers.

"Stella, over here. I'm over here."

Someone was here. At last. She must have arrived at the wrong entrance. She hurried toward the familiar voice trying to decide whom it sounded the most like. A masculine voice, but not old like Grandpa Jim's.

"I've been looking for you, Stella. I've been worried about you."

Someone cared about her. She broke into a jog. The only reason she committed suicide—besides escaping a terrible outcome—was that no one really cared about her. Her mother arguing with a crackpot minister made her wonder. Did she know anyone young who had died? There was that guy in high school who hung himself from the park swing set after his awkward prom date request. Not as if she could forget him, especially since some people believed her refusal spurred his actions. She hadn't said yes or no, just burst into tears.

Not a great memory, the only other person she knew who died was a transfer student in her math class. Someone mentioned he passed out walking home on a frosty night and froze to death after taking a handful of prescription drugs.

Maybe her version of the afterlife was only for people she knew that OD'd.

"To your right, Stella."

She peered into the darkness, trying to remember the boy's name. It would be good if she remembered it. His voice struck a responsive card indicating somehow that they were more connected than she remembered. Karl, something. Kev. Yeah, that was it, Kevin. Confident, she had his name. She turned into the darkness.

The creaking sound increased as a wind buffeted her, pushing her back.

"Stella, where are you going?" A note of fear tinged the question.

Oh my goodness, she had to get to Kevin, but the wind kept pushing her back. "Stop it!" she screamed the words, not expecting anything, but the wind vanished. Turning back to her path, she shouted, "I'm coming."

A small orb of light appeared growing larger as she stopped by a massive tree with something hanging from it. A body. Not again. Her feet remained mired in the mist as the body slowly rotated. This time Mitch looked fresher, his skin intact. His hanging happened recently.

Her hands pressed on her temples securing her head to her neck. Instead of devils with pitchforks, Hell was obviously a place where all her mistakes followed, denouncing her as the fraud she was. "How did this happen? My death was supposed to solve Cam harassing you."

Her fingers moved up into her hair, gripping it, pulling it. Tiny shards of physical pain joined her mental anguish as her eyes stayed on her friend swaying from the tree. Odd. He was almost like a decoration, an especially terrible one. He didn't even look dead, except for his face, which was ruddy and bruised. Maybe he wasn't dead yet. She could still save him. That was her mission to save Mitch. She was here in this misty between worlds place to save him. Here she thought she had no purpose in life, but this was it.

Her fingers dropped from her head, as a purpose grew inside her, rather like the ball of white light, she'd often visualize when covering herself with healing energy. The thought propelled her to the base of the tree trunk. Her right hand rested on the tree as she searched for a reachable branch. All of them hung out of reach. Even jumping wouldn't make her tall enough. How did people climb trees?

"Damn, why'd I have to be such a girly girl growing up? I should be able to climb this tree."

Mitch's laugh sounded behind her. "I'd like to see you climb a tree, but to what purpose. How would it change anything?"

Didn't he understand she was trying to save him and didn't have time for idle chitchat? Her eyes continued to search the tree for a possible handy built-in ladder as she spoke. Not looking at him made it easier to concentrate. "I'm trying to save you. If I can get up the tree, I can cut you down."

Squirrels climbed trees all the time. As far as she knew, they didn't have claws. A jump propelled her almost a foot off the ground as she flung her wide-spread fingers at the tree trunk. Her fingertips caught on the rough bark. Her heart leaped. She'd be able to crawl up the tree just like a squirrel or some macabre creature from a cut-rate horror movie. A snap had heralded the breaking of the bark before she fell with a sickening splat. Her hands were buried wrist deep in the mist. Still, she could feel something thick and moist under her fingertips. She pulled her hands up immediately, examining them for evidence of what she touched. A few long scratches with droplets of blood outlining them and a broken nail were the only evidence of her failed attempt. Apparently, squirrels were much lighter.

"Stella, what do you plan to do once you get up here? Are you going to gnaw through the rope with your teeth?"

Mitch's body twirled slightly, allowing her to see his face. He managed a brow lift as he faced her. Strange, the same facial expressions he'd use when he was alive. The familiar gesture exerted an emotional tug. She had to save him. Getting up became problematic since she didn't want to stick her hands back into the ground covering mist.

If she could stay disconnected from it, or as much as possible, it wouldn't absorb her. She wouldn't become part of the gloomy backdrop. Probably not feasible, but all she had to go on was instincts. Her hands rested on her knees as she leaned forward, pushing off her legs to stand. "I'm not giving up on you,

Mitch."

The words were as much for her as they were for him, a bit of a rallying cry. She wasn't sure how she'd save him unless she sprouted wings and developed scissor like teeth capable of chewing through the rope. Her feet shuffled back allowing her to get a better image of the tree. Huge. So big, that some of the thick branches dipped down to the ground.

Why hadn't she seen that before? She darted toward the low branches, not sure how she'd solve the cutting issue, but she had to try. The slender limbs touching the ground didn't look strong enough to hold her weight, but maybe they would. Her sudden speed burst should have carried her to the location, but the branches lifted, moving out of range again.

What? She blinked. Okay, she did take a bunch of drugs, and that might mess with her mind. There was also the possibility of torture in the afterlife. Trick playing trees could be part of the plan. The large, bare tree, she'd formerly regarded as simply dead, took on malevolent characteristics. She'd swear there were two evil eyes in the lines in the trunk, and a knothole created a slyly grinning mouth.

"Give it up. You're not helping yourself or me. We're both dead. You could have helped me earlier."

Her teeth sunk into her bottom lip as she listened.

"I know Cam had something on you. It had you running scared. You could have told me. Together, we could have worked something out." His concerned eyes held hers. His right arm stretched out with the palm up and open. His crooked little finger stood out awkwardly away from the rest of his fingers *reminding her of a kid not picked for the team, standing near the team, but not with them.*

Working in the computer lab provided either chaos that required more than the three workers they had or dead time. Her nose crinkled at the expression and swiftly corrected it. Empty hours didn't sound that much better. During this period, they exchanged stories about their childhoods. His crooked finger resulted from climbing a forbidden tree and falling. Despite the pain, he didn't inform his mother because that would mean confessing his disobedience. Besides, he didn't know it was broken. The pain, he figured, was a type of cosmic spanking.

The injured finger had blackened before his mother insisted on taking him to the doctor. X-rays showed that the break had already started healing crookedly. The only reasonable thing was to break it again and splint it, but, having already suffered through painful days and sleepless nights the idea had him whimpering. His strong reaction had his mother settling for antibiotics to help speed up the healing much to the doctor's disgust.

The finger identified him more than anything else could. It told her about his unwillingness to disappoint his family. His one DUI must have been devastating, the gift that kept on giving rather like an STD. Who knew Cam had a connection that allowed him to dig up the incident.

A silence hung thick between them. It both served as an invisible cord connecting them, and a wall. The blankness required an answer, a reply, some explanation. A crow called in the distance, causing an involuntary jump and a backward glance over her shoulder.

"There are crows here?"

Mitch's outstretch hand dropped to his side, with a floppy rubbery motion indicating no bone, no muscle, and no life.

"I asked why you couldn't confide in me, and you talk about crows? I thought we had something. I felt like you trusted me."

Each word pierced her skin like an icicle, searching for her heart. When the tip found the beating heart, then it would freeze solid. Stop that, you're already dead, nothing to freeze. The impression of wings had her ducking her head as a stately owl glided past her ear.

"Surprised you heard him coming. Most don't."

Her mind grabbed onto the word, most. That implied others walked through this misty shadowland stopping and talking to Mitch, who swung in the breeze similar to an oversized windsock.

"There are others here?"

She turned slowly regarding the bare trees with a suspicious gaze, expecting zombies half hidden by the trunks. First a crow, then an owl, what next? A vulture or a shambling cow carcass to remind her of her deceased state?

"You always changed the subject when I got too close to something you didn't want to talk about. I allowed it when we were both alive because I was too worried about you liking me. The wrong word or action would cause you to scurry away rather like a wild deer. There were times I thought we made a connection, but I must have been wrong."

Both his eyebrows lowered into a V as the wind spun his body, causing his words to trail after him. "Must have had a good laugh with Cam about me kissing you."

An uncomfortable thickness formed in her throat. A gulp didn't remove it. She swallowed again to no effect. Regret lingered in her esophagus blocking it worse than a wad of unchewed peanut butter sandwich. Her right hand went up to her chest as she coughed. What if she couldn't breathe? A rising panic raced through her. The hairs on her arm stood up as her senses responded in a fight or flight reaction she recognized from her physiology class. Who knew the same physical responses happened after death too.

Think. Nothing can hurt you here since you're already dead. A raucous unfamiliar bird call drew her attention upward. Two large birds flew in a circle their skinny necks standing out in contrast to their thick-feathered bodies, too big for crows and definitely not eagles. The croaking cry came again, chilling her while drawing on a memory. Two similar birds had crouched close to the entrance of their gated subdivision tearing way at a dead doe. Her father had told her to look away as he made the turn, but she had looked back instead, curious to see what he didn't want her to see.

One bird had plunged his curved beak into the rotting carcass while the other cackled in anticipation. Bile had risen in her throat causing her to bolt from the car when it stopped in front of their house.

"Vultures," Mitch spat the word in disgust. "Means I don't have much time left. They show up this time every day to do

their dirty work. A tidying of the premises."

Vultures ate dead animals. Her father had explained it to her after she emptied her stomach. It was nature's way. This revelation only assured her that nature had a dark side. A sudden screech preceded the vulture's downward plunge. Stella dropped to the ground and covered her head certain the birds would go for her eyes. Isn't that what they did in the movies?

"Get back! Stop it! Not again!"

Hearing Mitch's agonized cries, she dropped her arms. His body swung wildly as the birds took turns diving at him, ripping off flesh in the process. His legs kicked ineffectually at the determined scavengers. A large hole in his side exposing muscle, a rib, and what she thought, might be the liver. The only liver she ever looked at belonged to the cat she dissected in biology. A uniform gray colored all the feline's organs, making the lab difficult.

Her hand wrapped around a nearby branch. She swung it, using it as a sword, screaming as she charged the birds. They flew a short distance and huddled in a nearby tree, shrieking their complaints.

"Thanks. Appreciate your effort. They'll be back. It happens this way every day. Rather like the Prometheus myth. Instead of my liver, they devour all of me. Each day, my flesh returns and once again I become the human piñata."

His wound didn't ooze blood, but an organ slid a little, threatening to spill out on the ground near her feet. Thank the Goddess it didn't. Her gaze moved upward gliding over the missing chunks of flesh and ripped clothing. Dark splotches covered his face, and his skin tightened against his skull giving him the look of a dried apple doll with severe, mournful features. His thin barely there lips pulled away from his teeth in a parody of a horse grin.

She shouted over the vultures' vocalizing. "What can I do to help you?"

His breath came out in a wheezy gasp, "Too late...to...help... Did you care...for me a little?"

It wasn't supposed to be happening this way. Her death should have put everything back in balance. All would be as it should be, not like this. A pair of vicious, ugly creatures should not devour the only dependable male she knew. The birds' complaints rose in volume along with the noise of hundreds of beating wings. A flock of vultures darkened the sky, making the shadowy landscape into instant night. A sickening odor of death and decaying flesh landed with them as many perched in nearby trees and several on the ground beside her feet.

One pecked at her foot between the sandal straps, punctur-ing it. Blood decorated the wound exciting the birds. The dark harbingers crowded forward. She stumbled backwards in her attempt to escape.

"Run! I'll distract them." Mitch thrashed about sending a foot flying in the process. The birds lighted on it screaming insults as they shoved each other out of the way with their strong wings. "Hurry, Stella. You have to complete your soul's mission."

Soul's mission. What did he mean? "Mitch, I hate leaving you. The kiss mattered a great deal."

A large vulture's wingspan hid Mitch's face, cut off a reply that started with "Stella, I'll always—", and ended it with an ominous gurgle.

CHAPTER TEN

R UN, RUN, RUN, the words repeated in her mind. *Her feet carried her away from the sound of the feeding frenzy. The path veered to the right but hadn't she come that way? Why bother returning to where she'd already been. No door awaited her, allowing her the ability to go back to life for an instant do-over. Too bad, since suicide provided no solution at all. It only made everything worse.*

Another path cut through the bare tree woods a little further up to her left. A stitch in her side gave a moment for contemplation as she gulped air and shoved her fingers into the spasm. The trees resembled a clutch of black-garbed widows huddled together and away from the path. A dark glossy shrubbery peeked out of the ground fog. Strange. She hadn't seen this before. It looked like it could be alive, unlike the trees.

Even though she could no longer hear the vultures, it didn't mean they weren't there. No doubt, they'd be looking for the second course in a couple of minutes. Besides, bushes couldn't look ominous. Better hurry. She broke into a jog, heading toward the glossy leaf bushes. The ground mist cleared, exposing a gravel path and a rabbit. The black and white rabbit resembled an overfed pet rather than a resident of a haunted forest. It stood on its hind legs, almost reaching Stella's knees.

His nose twitched as his mouth moved. She expected it to speak. Leah had followed a rabbit to her grandfather in her time traveling experience. Could Leah's grandfather have sent the rabbit as a messenger? Made sense since the grandfather's last name was Hare. Weren't rabbits symbols of luck? How would anyone know she needed help since she hadn't shared her plans?

The rabbit's dark eyes brimmed with intelligence or so she thought. "Speak to me." Instead of the furry little mouth opening to complain about being late and missing tea as in the popular child's book, nothing. No words about turning left at the next hanging corpse emerged from his mouth. Its cheeks continued moving as if it had some massive wad of gum. No words. How frustrating! The first semi-normal creature was no help at all.

Know and be known. *The cryptic words materialized in her mind, pushing out any reference to children's books and forest creatures with no sense of direction.* Know and be known. *The words came again in clear bell-like sounds. The rabbit continued chewing without a glimmer of teeth showing, obviously not talking.*

Know and be known. *The words rose in volume the speaker shouted over her warring thoughts, fears, and reflections on childhood reading selections. The bunny gave her a reproachful look as if animals were capable of such a thing. It dropped to four legs and bounced off into the mist.*

The fog grew thick, rising quickly, covering the path and the direction of the rabbit. Her eyes searched for the hare as she lunged in the direction it went. Her only chance of leaving hopped away twitching its tail. A sense of urgency propelled her right into the glossy bushes, which happened to have thorns on them. The brambles held her tight as she struggled to free herself. What were the bushes doing in the path?

The more she struggled, the tighter the branches wrapped around her squeezing her tight, thorns penetrating her skin. The bush belonged in a horror movie where plants grabbed at people and sometimes ate them. She swallowed hard. As a light snack for some aggressive shrubbery, she'd never complete her soul mission, whatever that was.

What did they do in the movies when attacked by plants? Sure, problem-solving using hackneyed movie plots might not be the best plan, but what else was there? In the movies, the person usually had a machete to hack off limbs. Yeah, made the mistake of dying without taking a weapon with her. No wonder ancient burials featured weapons placed with the body. They knew something modern man forgot.

Death was not the great sleep nor was it a marble condominium in the clouds. Who knew it would be some never-ending scavenger hunt with meaningless clues. Know and be known, *how would that help her with this mutant plant? The glossy leaf plant looked benign, however, was anything but. Delicately grabbing a branch, she detangled the needle-like thorns from her clothing only to have another twig wrap around her. So much for stealth. The plant knew what she was doing before she did it. Leah's Nana, Esmeralda, always talked to the plants because she credited them with intelligence and under-*

standing.

"Um, plant, could you please let me go?" Her voice echoed in the stillness, sounding both loud and stupid. As a reply, the branches wrapped around her left knee tightened, the thorns penetrated the thin material, embedding into the sensitive skin behind her knee.

"Ow!" She glanced down at the limb wrapped around her knee like a tourniquet. "Just my luck to score the plant bully. Do you want to play rough, huh? Take this."

Her fingers grabbed a fist full of leaves, jerking upward. A high keen filled the air as the ragged edges of the torn leaves spurted black liquid. A spattering of black dots decorated the front of her dress. Creepy. Did the plant actually scream and could the liquid be blood, well plant blood? Never had that happen back in the real world. Her legs were still captive, but the grip eased off some.

Her hands hovered over the plant before plunging into greenery ripping wildly. The high-pitched screams stopped her for a moment. "It's you or me, plant," she growled the words through gritted teeth as she continued plucking. The thorns tore at her skin, causing numerous scratches and bleeding. Dark red blood slithered down her hands mixing with the black liquid from the plant.

In vampire movies, the mingling of blood would cause the sharing of consciousness. That's how they tracked Dracula by using Mina Harker's impressions of where the master vampire resided. Did she really want to know what a plant was thinking?

Stop. The plaintive plea sounded in her head. Without any

actual thought, she did stop. The bare bush sported only a few leaves, a multitude of thorns, and oozing black liquid slid over it dripping into the vapor. Great Goddess, she killed it or close to it. The branches that held her tight draped uselessly on top of her feet. How long had she kept at it after the plant gave up?

Leaves stuck out of her balled fists. Her fingers unbent, revealing the torn fragments. She hadn't meant to kill it. It was either it or her. Her actions were instinctive. What anyone would do to survive, right? She took one ragged leaf and held it up to the branch. The torn leaf adhered to the branch with the ripped part growing back before her eyes. Talk about regeneration. She repeated the operation with a half dozen leaves but then stopped.

No reason to give the plant enough energy to attack again. The rest of the leaves fluttered toward the ground from her outstretched fingers. Their slow, graceful tumble ended when she could no longer see them in the mist. A slight movement in her peripheral vision caused her to pivot to her left. The torn leaves were silently marching up the branches similar to ants on parade and reconnecting. The sight had mesmerized her for a second before she bolted back to the path.

A thick hedge blocked her original path. Another passageway opened, complete with glowing moonflowers lighting the way with their open white blossoms similar to morning glories. Would it be smart to choose the easy path? Might as well have a neon sign with an arrow on it. A dangerous shrub behind her that could pull up roots and follow determined her choice. Best bet would be to get out of the angry plant's vicinity.

Besides the flowers didn't appear to have any murderous intents, but then she'd thought that about the bush. The mists obscured the path, and then pulled back enough revealing a few feet. The vapor floated higher encompassing her in thick fog, reminding her of cotton batting as it wrapped around her. Warm, soft, and possibly suffocating her, but that would only apply if she were still alive.

Her initial struggle only tightened the white blanket around her. Violence is never an answer. The mantra popped into her mind probably from an anti-bullying campaign. Yeah, right, easy to say when something isn't trying to absorb or possibly digest you. *Inhaling deeply, she took two deep meditative breaths, grounding herself. Her panic lessened as she used the meditation chant.*

Acknowledge it; let it go, be at peace. *She inhaled deeply once more aware that calmness flowed through her, relaxing her muscles, gliding over her skin, penetrating deep in her psyche. It reminded her of water supporting her, floating on a raft in the pool with not a care in the world. Didn't people use white light in visualization? Sure, her light had weight and texture.*

For a moment, she drifted above the trees, peering down at the white encased figure on the path. The mummy-like creature was she, but she felt no fear or even attachment to the form. In the distance, mountains welled up out of the mist projecting both grandeur and ominousness. An understanding slipped over her. The faraway mountains were her end destination. As soon as the epiphany occurred, she landed back in her mist-wrapped body. The whiteness no longer frightened her.

A slightly off-key singing drifted on the air. The song, an old rock ballad about not stopping, reminded her of something her mother might have sung before she found religion. The singer stumbled over a few lyrics and inserted dubious ones of her making. Just like her mother. The dark forest grew thinner, giving over to spindly pine trees and large boulders. A woman in leggings, a tulle ballerina skirt and a fuchsia off the shoulder top strummed a guitar. A green scrunchie decorated her asymmetrical ponytail, which bobbed in time with the few notes she picked out on the guitar.

Something familiar about the outfit and the woman tugged at her memory. At least, she wasn't swinging from a noose. A live person suited her much better than the talking dead. It inspired less guilt too. Perhaps feeling her scrutiny, the woman glanced up and grinned.

"I bet you think I'm a lousy guitar player. I am." A carefree laugh bubbled up full of joy and abandonment.

Stella caught herself laughing with her. What a relief to meet someone happy on this soul mission. "No worries. I can't play either, but I always wanted to learn."

"You still can." The woman offered the advice with a strong pluck. The discordant note hung in the air, confirming her inability.

"Yeah, I know, but…" She hesitated, not knowing if she should add, but I'm dead. Who knew what people or souls did after they die? Plenty of people with agendas would tell you in a heartbeat. Personally, she didn't care for any of the final solutions.

The woman rested the guitar against the rock, pushed off, and stood. "Hey, I'm Roberta. Most people call me Bobby."

"Hi, Bobby." She grasped her outstretched hand and shook it firmly. The warm, solid clasp of a hand anchored her in the moment. Her lips tugged up in response to Bobby's almost constant smile. The journey wouldn't be too stressful if everyone else were this nice. Apparently, Bobby would give her some cosmic clue or insight to complete her mission. Her bottom teeth scraped over her top lip with just enough pressure to let her know both were there. No body parts falling off yet.

A person didn't just ask how long someone had been dead. Not sure, what protocol was in this nebulous place. "Cool outfit you got on there. Vintage?" Stella asked carefully.

Bobby fingered her puffy skirt. "Oh, vintage, if you mean banging,' it is. I got it the other day. It's part of my college wardrobe." She spun in a fast turn with her arms gracefully over her head. "The whole outfit makes me feel just like Cyndi Lauper, except I can't sing or play the guitar."

"Cyndi who?" Bobby might as well be speaking a foreign language. Should she know this person? The same feeling of bewilderment she normally experienced when the fantasy role-play gamers tried to talk about their avatars and adventures swept over Stella. They assumed wrongly because she worked in the computer lab that she must be interested in online RPGs too. Instead of chiming into the conversation, she found something to do in the lab, which kept her from acting similar to an amnesiac or a Droid missing a memory chip.

Bobby blinked twice before breaking into an upbeat song

about girls wanting to have fun. It sounded familiar. Maybe Stella had heard it on a television show or movie. Wait. Her mother used to sing it when they were at the park playground. She'd push Stella in the swing and sing while other mothers screamed toothless threats at their children as they climbed the slide the wrong way or threw sand at one another. At the time, she'd thought her mother made up the song just for her, especially since she only sang the chorus.

Bobby danced closer, still singing, and grabbed her hands, swinging her in a slow circle. The unexpected action caught Stella by surprise, but she found her balance fast enough not to stumble again as they reeled in some 80's flavored version of Ring around the Rosey. The nagging feeling she should know this cheerful female reasserted itself. Obviously, it would help with the soul mission. Their spinning circle wobbled as Bobby leaned back a couple inches too far, taking them both down.

The soft green grass cushioned their fall. The mist had vanished, and the dark woods had turned into a green, inviting copse with sunlight streaming through the leaves. The rocks and the mountains remained, along with a laughing Bobby.

Odd that everything changed. Why did it change? Bobby dropped her hands and pushed herself up. "I wish you were my roommate."

"Really?" Happiness arced through her body that someone wanted her as a roommate. Being from different times could be a barrier. "I wish you were mine. The one I had was like a cranky iguana slithering in, making noise, eating my food, and them slithering out with some caustic jab."

"Yeah. She sounds like a winner. Didn't catch your name?" Bobby arched an eyebrow as she dusted off her leggings and picked a twig out of her skirt.

"Stella." She paused waiting for the inevitable wrong name. Estelle, Estella, even Estrella, a few even tried to change her name to Ellie, which she'd admit was more playful, but it wasn't her name. She watched her fellow traveler shape the words first, as she made her way over to what she knew would be a warmed rock. The uniform heat of the boulder encouraged Stella to stretch out putting her hands behind her head, staring up at the bright blue sky. Too bright, she closed her eyes, soaking in the warmth.

"Stella. I like that name. Not common, ya know."

"Yeah," she agreed, not opening her eyes. It'd be nice if she could just stay in this part of her journey. Once grade school started, there were very few visits to the park. Instead, her mother carted her around to half dozen classes where she learned manners, gymnastics, and languages. Being able to say, "Where is the American Embassy?" in Russian and Italian ended up serving no purpose. She could have been outside soaking up the sun instead of math tutoring to make sure she excelled in school.

"Probably because they didn't want their baby girls associated with that female traitor in that old play."

Stella opened her eyes, realizing she never gave much thought to her name. Once, she looked it up online, and it meant Star, which she thought was cool. "What female traitor? What play?" Her gaze scanned the immediate area for Bobby. Nothing. She jackknifed into a sitting position. Where was she?

"Bobby?" she called, hating the slight note of hysteria in the *single word. Why did she think dying would be a long dreamless sleep? So far, it had been more work, worry, and downright creepiness than living.*

"Here."

The voice came from below her. Stella peered over the edge of the boulder. An audible sigh of relief escaped her lips upon spotting her companion. Bobby had her face in a large patch of yellow daffodils crowded together. The flowers, which muffled her words, Stella would swear hadn't been there before. How could you miss all that yellow?

"I love Daffodils. They're my favorite flowers."

"They're my mother's favorite too, which surprised me."

"Hmm, why?" Bobby rocked back on her heels and stared up at Stella. "Why wouldn't she love daffodils? They're both beautiful and courageous. They come up before any other flowers. Sure that spring is here. They are the optimist of flowers. Their bright yellow color makes me think of sunshine and happiness. They endure year after year." Throwing her hands skyward, she announced with enthusiasm, "The daffodil is my role model. Forget people. Maybe we should model ourselves after plants. Much less drama. Whadya think?"

Plants as role models? Well, that's something she never considered before. "Yeah, I guess it could work. A plant does what it is supposed to do until it dies. Daffodils would be better than most people I know."

"Exactly." Bobby's laughter bubbled out of her as easy as breathing. Stella envied her. Too much time went into weighing if she should laugh at something. Would she offend someone if she laughed? Was it politically correct? Should she laugh even though she thought it was rather mean spirited? In the end, the

opportunity usually passed her by before she could decide. Wasn't laughter a reaction as opposed to a choice?

The bubbly blonde-haired woman stood and leaned against the stone just brushing Stella's leg. Greedy for human contact, she moved her leg the barest millimeter keeping the contact. "If daffodils aren't your mother's type of flower, what would be?"

Good question. "Something, dark, and broody, that does well in the shade. A navy or black rose bud that never blooms out fully."

"Sounds terrible. Is she really that bad?" she asked, screwing up her face in a grimace.

Depending on her mother's mood, sometimes she not only became the dark rain cloud, but the lightning and thunder too. "Not always. Mainly, she's sad, disappointed in life. My father left for another woman. Just walked out of our lives one day. Most people say they know it's going to happen, but my mom didn't. Why else would she react so negatively? Huge scene in front of the neighbors."

"Bummer. Should have known. Did she get up, dust herself off, and vow to make your father pay?"

Her cupped palms held Stella's attention as she analyzed Bobby's statement. Her jaw clicked as she worked it around. The clicking came from it not being out of alignment. The dentist accused her of grinding her teeth at night. Try living with the constant pressure of two adults playing an oversized emotional game of Jenga. The blocks had to come tumbling down sometimes.

She yawned on purpose, fighting the desire to grind her teeth. "At first, she was bitter, and then she became all depressed. I even missed her bossiness. Then she joined some church that told her what to do and think. The pastor's a total douchebag. Hate him." She slammed her balled fist into her other hand in a hollow slap for emphasis.

"Do you not like this pastor, then?" Bobby turned a mischievous expression her way. Stella sent her a dark glance, earning laughter. "Well, did you consider maybe your mother needed someone to tell her what to do? Maybe she didn't trust her own judgment since things went so wrong."

It made sense. Not the type of sense, Stella liked, though. Her parents were supposed to be all-knowing people who provided stability in her life. Her father humiliated her by hooking up with a woman young enough to be her older sister. He'd turned into a stereotype of a middle-aged man trying to recapture his youth. Her mother turned to religion, perhaps imagining it would solve all her problems if she just followed the right rules and gave enough money to the church.

"No, never considered it. My mom used to have it together. She was an office manager that managed other people's schedules. Very organized. Prompt. Efficient."

"Sounds like a control freak."

"She was."

"What happens when a control freak can't control something?"

"They go crazy?" Her mother had lost touch with reality.

Instead of her usual smile, Bobby's expression took on the thousand-yard stare. She sighed deeply. "I'm not sure how your mother dealt. All the super organization was a coping mechanism. I read about it once. People try to control their surroundings, since they can't control life."

Oddly, this person who never met her mother might have a

point. Stella's lips twisted to one side as she imagined her mother as a panicked engineer of an out of control locomotive. "There wasn't too much she could do. Everything happened all at once, too, losing her job, losing her husband, and then, I went off to college. Maybe it was easier to give the responsibility of her life over to some scheming religious huckster who saw a tool."

A discordant chord filled the air. Bobby had the guitar tucked under one arm again, strummed the chords, and sang slightly off key, "There once was a woman named." She paused, angling her head in Stella's direction. "What was your mom's name again?"

"Roberta, like yours." Didn't she mention this before or did she just think it? Couldn't remember what she thought or did. Was this part of crossing over, the forgetting?

"Hmm, strange." Her fingers plucked the strings creating a trio of notes, not harmonious ones. "Imagine she didn't go for any nicknames like Robby or Bob, huh?"

The thought of her efficient mother sporting a nickname was unthinkable. Her father never used any endearments for her mother, always calling her Roberta, more like she was an acquaintance or co-worker he didn't know too well, or maybe didn't want to know.

A few more chords had sounded before Bobby settled on one she liked and continued strumming. "Roberta, Roberta, where are you now? You journey far and long with no clear destination. Tired and weary, you closed your eyes and woke up to a world strange to you."

The words could have applied to her as well as her mother. "Hey, that's decent considering you made it up on the spot."

Holding the guitar close with one arm, Bobby cupped her

right hand and polished her fingers on her shirt. "Yeah, I have a few talents. Making up stuff is one of them."

"No, it was more than made up." This throwback to the seventies described the situation perfectly. "I don't know a whole lot about my parents, but I did know they got married because my mom was pregnant with me. I ended up tying together two people never meant to be together in a loveless marriage."

A snort, slightly animal-like, came from her companion. "Seriously, who told you that BS?"

"Well, uh, my father right before he left."

Bobby grimaced. "The crap people tell their children in an effort to whitewash their actions makes me want to barf." She accompanied the statement with a gagging reaction. "Tell me you didn't fall for it."

Her silence served as answer enough. Bobby put her guitar down and wrapped an arm around Stella's shoulders. "Okay. Let's look at things realistically. They both had choices. Hadn't they heard of The Pill? So they got married, a choice they both made. At any time, they could have called it quits. They didn't. Then your father decides to jump ship. He somehow tried to place his guilt and shame on the only person who didn't have a choice in the scenario. Lame."

The arm across her shoulder comforted her as much as the words did. When the same thoughts had occurred to her, she'd rejected them as an easy way out of the cesspool her family had become. Bobby could be right. If she were right, then her dying didn't help her family or Mitch. An impulse, a push, had her standing and looking off in the distance at the mountains. Her time here was up. Bobby didn't know because she continued chattering.

"I wouldn't put up with settling down and being the traditional wifey. No not me, I want to travel, explore, and have adventures."

Bobby was her mother. She knew it. This carefree, happy girl caved into pressure to be something she wasn't. The epiphany had her staring, cataloging the outfit, even her attitude. So different from her mother who could have popped out of a filing cabinet fully formed and attired in a washable suit and sensible shoes.

The glade darkened. Gathered clouds minimized the sunlight while an ominous dampness seeped out of the ground developing into a mist. Not a good sign. Time to go. She glanced back, wanting to remember the free-spirited version of her mother, but the outspoken Bobby had disappeared.

In the distance, the sun shone down on a slender path similar to the outlined route on a GPS. Leaving no doubt, in which direction she'd go with no reason to look behind and no desire to repeat everything she'd already done. Bobby's mellow personality appealed, which was weird considering she'd never gotten along with her mother.

CHAPTER ELEVEN

*T*HE DARKNESS AND *mist increased, causing her to break into a jog. No low-lying briars reached for her feet. Still, no reason to linger or take chances. The universe, God, Goddess, whatever created this world, urged her to move on. A meadow with tall, waving grass starting to turn brown, indicating fall or approaching winter, stood in front of the mountains.*

Dust kicked up around her sandals as she walked. Exhaustion dogged her steps until moving became more like walking through a pool. It shouldn't be this hard. Sleep would be nice. Yes, that's what she needed. A green mossy area beckoned in the sea of dry grass. Odd, it would exist, but it did. Her feet headed toward the soft looking mound when a voice sounded in her head. Don't stop. Don't sleep. You'll never awake.

What? Stella's determined march to the mound halted. She turned slowly looking for anyone or anything that could be talking to her. Never underestimate the plants or the wildlife in this strange, unknown landscape of nothing, except for the grass, soft looking moss, and mountains. Did she think it? It didn't make sense because she wanted to sleep and wouldn't warn herself not to. Sleeping sounded wonderful. Sure, a feather pillow would be nice, but she'd settle for the moss. A large pillow stuffed inside a crisp white case appeared on top of the mound.

Exactly what she needed. Ah, sleep, wonderful sleep. Three strides carried her to the moss mound where she fell to her knees. Her fingertips glided across the ironed pillowcase. It felt real but needed further investigation. Her head rested on the case. The scent of fresh cotton and the lingering aroma of spray starch relaxed her. Nice. She rolled onto her back thinking how the pillow reminded her of the ones from home. The cases her mother painstakingly starched and ironed. Once she told Leah about her mother's need to iron almost anything, she could drape over an ironing board. Instead of making a caustic remark as she expected, Leah's lips turned up in an uncertain smile, the kind people give when they had no real answer and are unsure what's expected.

Yeah, she didn't know what she expected her friend to say. Truth told she liked the ironed pillowcases. So smooth and cool against her skin, her eyelids closed as she promised herself she'd only take a small break, a tiny nap, that's all.

Get up! *The shrieked words rattled inside her skull, forcing her eyes open with a snap. Now, she knew she didn't do that because all she wanted was to sleep.*

Another voice choked with tears, more distant, called her name. Stella, Stella, my precious child stay with me.

Her mother, she was almost sure of it. Not the happy, care-free version, but the ironing one. Was she here? Sitting up, Stella looked around. No one, but the ground fog and darkness were closer than before and moving fast. If she stayed asleep, it would cover her in a matter of minutes. Not an outcome she wanted.

The vapor swirled around as in dancing, retreating, and then swirling forward fooling her into thinking it wasn't moving fast. It was.

Decision made; she pushed up into a standing position. Her legs moved in rhythm with her swinging arms, similar to a race walker. The strappy sandals she'd donned earlier with high hopes of a romantic lunch with Cam did not serve. They alternated between separating her little toe from the rest of her toes and sliding across the terrain. Her feet slick with dust stuck out of the front of the sandals catching every broken stick and stray stone. Pain pulsed through her big toe as it encountered a pointed shard. Her lips mashed together as she held in her yelp.

Hadn't every childhood book and its movie counterpart featured dark woods where bad things happen? Leah's Nana explained that the dark represented the unknown, not necessarily evil. So far, the unknown hadn't treated her well. Frustrated with her sandals, she stopped for a moment, ripping them off her feet and throwing them into the tall grass. Without them, she could move faster.

The unwelcome sensation moved over her like anonymous hands touching her in a crowd, when her arms were pinned against her body, and she could do nothing about it. Afraid to look over her shoulder, she kept going forward, breaking into a light jog. Wincing whenever her feet stepped on a stone or stick, which was more than she liked. It sounded like someone was behind her, but she didn't want it to be true.

The sound of grass brushing against jean-clad legs came closer. Not Bobby, she knew that much. Please don't let it be

Mitch, too macabre. The footsteps broke into a run making Stella erupt into a lope, scoping the area for a possible hiding place. Pain pierced her side making her wonder why her lack of athleticism stayed with her even after death. Labored breathing contributed to her dry mouth and inability to swallow. How long could she go on like this? Almost anyone could outrun her half-loping, half-limping gait.

Wasn't death supposed to be easy? Pain-free? Wasn't that why people committed suicide? What a crock! Someone needed to come back and explain that things weren't exactly peaceful on the other side. The grass crackled behind her, underneath a heavy footfall. Heavy breathing, not her own, reached her ears. So close. Help me now, Goddess. *An extra burst of energy sent her speeding down the trail. Must get away.*

"Stella."

Her name caught and stayed in the wind. A familiar, mas-culine voice, not Mitch. She stopped, even though everything inside her warned her not to and turned fearing what she'd find. Cam's bowed head greeted her as he rested his hands on his bent knees trying to catch his breath.

He glanced up, pinning her with his gaze. Before the same look would have mesmerized her. Now, it frightened her, making her back up slowly. Same artistically ruffled hair, primo bod, and model worthy skin, but it had no effect on her. No desire to look at him in awe, wondering how he could have chosen her. No, the mixture of lust and pride went missing. Maybe death did that to a person, but she remembered still caring about Mitch, even her mother.

Cam elicited none of these feelings, only the desire to get away from him before he contaminated her with his brand of evilness. Turning her back to him, she fixed her eyes on the mountains and continued her journey.

"What are you doing? Why won't you wait for me?"

Her pace slowed. Leaving him would be rude. The memory of his intentions to ruin Mitch if she didn't fix his grades resulted in her speeding up again.

"Wait, you worthless ho."

Seriously? He thought that would make her stop. A small rock on the ground beckoned her without a word. It fit into her hand exactly as she thought it would. Pivoting, she released it toward her intended target only to have it skim Cam's shoulder.

"Hell. Have you lost your mind?"

His comment made her angry enough to scan the ground for more stones. Why did he keep following her? Was she crazy? Some people would say she was since she killed herself. It would make sense to some, especially everyone in her mother's fire and brimstone church. Crazy people did insane stuff. What was the definition of insanity? Dr. Poli, the chemistry prof, quoted Einstein's definition about once a week, something about doing the same thing and expecting different results. The quote could shame or enlighten those who never studied, but still expected to pass the weekly quiz.

Oh, she studied for the tests and aced most of them. Still, she expected Cam to be something he wasn't. He never showed any signs he was a stand up kind of person, just the opposite. His hand landed on her shoulder; she tried to shake it off, but it *remained, fingers digging into her collarbone.*

She stiffened her other hand and brought it down on his wrist as hard as she could breaking his hold. Cam swore and stumbled backward.

Stella glared at him. "I'm crazy all right. Crazy to think you were a decent human. Insane to believe you cared about me. Totally whacked because I thought you'd let me into your self-centered world. I was wrong. Dead wrong. I'd had enough of you when I was alive." She stomped her bare foot on the dusty path and fisted her hands.

The patronizing smile indicated he considered her words a show, the type of emotional upheaval females were prone to. His smug expression sent her blood rushing through her body as if she were a cartoon thermometer. Any time, she'd blow her top, and it would all go spurting out, except she wasn't a cartoon and nothing about the situation was funny.

"I'm done with you. Be gone." She clapped her hands in front of his face; the same way she'd treat a stray she didn't want to follow her.

His eyebrows lifted as his mouth dropped open. Her not wanting him shocked him more than any words and it was probably hard for him to conceive of any female not wanting him. She expected him to declare her a lesbian to soothe his ego. The rebuttal she expected never came. His surprised expression never changed as he grew lighter and lighter until she could see the outline of the darkening glade behind him.

Stella blinked twice. No Cam. Impressions from his distinctive athletic shoes remained on the dusty path, but he didn't. An initial curl of unease slowly unrolled through her body. Did she do that?

Her gaze went to the path and Cam's footprints, the only evidence he was ever there. Her head slowly shook side to side. He could have left on his own, but Cam never did things that didn't benefit Cam. The fact she wanted him gone would be reason enough to stay. This soul search stuff would be much easier on her own. On her own. The words echoed in her head as she pivoted toward the mountains.

"All on my own," she whispered the words afraid she might be overheard. Strange, yeah, she knew it. Stranger was her constant effort not to be alone. As an only child, she didn't come into the world with instant playmates. Instead, her mother made play dates, enrolled her in programs while constantly reminding her to play nice, which she soon discovered meant tamp down her feelings and go along with what the other child wanted. Her early experience of trying to assert her preferences was slapped down fast.

Her easing fear allowed her to remember the repressed memory. Normally she hid the memory in a box wrapped with yellow and black tape bearing the label, bad memory. The scent of finger paint tickled her nostrils while the sound of children laughing filled her ears in preschool. She recognized the pink housekeeping area. Pink to remind the girls that was their place, not the block center, or the car area with the rug printed with roads and cities.

Lilly, the beribboned daughter of a physician, elbowed Stella. "Let's play shopping."

Eli and Malcolm building a brightly colored city from blocks appealed more. Her slowness at replying earned her another elbow jab and redirection. "You can be the store owner."

Shopping was a tedious game, and being the storekeeper was even worse. It consisted of handing several items to Lilly while she complained they weren't what she wanted. Most of the time, Stella could never find anything that suited Lily, not a fun scenario.

Her mother wanted her to play with Lily, commenting that it would result in good connections. Spending more time with Lily sounded like torture. She tried to explain it to her mother, who laughed and told her to play nice.

With no freedom of choice, she'd handed Lily a faded dress that she'd discarded with a sniff. Her aggravation emerged in a sly manner. Stella knew her role. What if she changed it?

Lilly donned the sequined princess dress smoothing it over her body in front of the unbreakable mirror. Before she could complain about the dress, Stella spoke, remembering the attendant's words from the other day when her mother popped into an upscale fashion store.

"No, that dress does not suit. Take it off. Your skin and hair clash with it." She wasn't sure what clash meant, but she injected the same snootiness in her voice that the attendant used. Lilly erupted into loud sobs. It ended with the pre-school teacher scolding Stella and calling her mother.

Compromise was how to play the game, her mother explained after a lengthy timeout. The unfamiliar word must mean allowing other people to have their way. Often people were still mean even when they had their way. Her inability to tolerate stupid people made her a better, stronger scholar, but it left her feeling as if something was missing.

Patches of grass taking over the path ahead of her made her wonder if she'd veered off somewhere, but no clearer path presented itself. Of course, she had no clue where she was going or what would be there. The thought wasn't as horrifying as it would have been.

"The only thing that was missing was your own sense of self-worth." The remark startled her, although Leah had said as much.

Someone was walking next to her. Uncertain of the identity of the fellow traveler, Stella cut her eyes toward the stranger, trying not to be too obvious. An older woman with graying curls nodded in her direction. The woman's hand curled around a carved walking stick topped with a glass orb. The staff would be something Leah's grandmother would use, but the sizable stick measured close to six foot. Too big, even for the feisty Esmeralda Hare. Trying not to look or react, she took in her visitor's broomstick skirt and a flowing embroidered blouse, which told her nothing. The woman could be from almost any time and several regions. Her feet were bare too. Her green eyes reflected amusement. "Got any theories yet?"

"Are you my grandmother I never met?" She'd always wanted one. Someone preferably like Leah's who could give her counsel and gift her with a magickal charm or two.

The woman used her stick as a third leg creating a slightly odd gait. Stick, foot, foot, and stick again, the stick pulled her along. Stella slowed her pace out of consideration. The woman winked at her. "I saw what you did there. I'm not your grandmother, but a guide, even a mentor of sorts."

Stella stumbled to a stop. Her mouth dropped in surprise, then closed as she formulated a response. "A mentor! A guide! You're too late. I'm dead."

The rude words elicited a chuckle from the woman. "I'm glad you're finally finding your voice. We have much to talk about, you and me. Let's go to my house."

She pointed over Stella's shoulder. There was nothing behind her, but mountains. Five seconds ago, they filled the horizon. Doubting her senses, Stella pivoted slowly looking in the direction the woman pointed.

A small cottage with blue shutters and a purple door sat about hundred yards away. Some feathery wildflowers grew near the door, and an oversized Calico cat stretched out on a paving stone in the sun's rays. Smoke curled out of the chimney making it look almost storybook-like.

"Ah, you see it now. We only see what we allow ourselves to see." The woman nodded, planting her stick in front of her as she strode. "Your third eye is opening."

Stella placed her fingers on her forehead. The skin itched and twitched. Something was trying to break out of her skin. She'd heard plenty of talk about third eyes in Leah's house, but she assumed it meant something other than looking like a mythological creature.

The woman snorted, an inelegant almost bear like growl,

and then faced her with a grin. "Name's Maja. If you don't know your mythology, I was the most beautiful of the Pleiades sisters. Some folks changed my name and story, but I prefer Maja."

Her shoulders went up in a casual shrug as if being a mythological entity was no big deal. Stella mentally cataloged her companion's attributes, trying to decide if any were god-like. Maja towered over Stella, but she didn't intimidate with her presence. Tall, slender, she must be strong to carry such a massive walking stick.

The sleeping cat awoke at their approach, stretched, arching its back and morphing into a much larger, more lethal feline. Stella's skin around her eyes stretched at the sight of the sleek, muscled leopard. The large creature bounded forward, which resulted in Stella stumbling sideways as the graceful cat placed his front paws on Maja's shoulders, greeting her with a swipe of his long tongue.

Maja's husky laughter at the display settled the issue of her divine origins. No regular woman could hold up under the weight of a two-hundred pound plus pet, especially one in motion, which would quadruple the mass. What was the formula for force again?

"Come, Stella, stop thinking about math formulas and have some tea." Maja pushed the leopard down and gestured to her home, walking faster and more upright than before.

Weird, but Stella tabled her desire to ask about it. You didn't question the immortals.

The leopard resumed its cat shape and weaved in and out of

Stella's legs making her step carefully, unsure when she might find herself riding the large cat during an unexpected shapeshift.

Maja ducked as she entered the small cottage, making her wonder why the woman didn't whip up something larger. Inside, sunlight beamed through the windows in squares of illumination in the dim cottage, and a fire glowed in the fireplace. Intricate tapestries decorated the wall depicting stories she assumed were mythological in nature. Hard to tell in the light, but one featured a bear who turned into a man. Hope there wouldn't be a quiz later.

Two overstuffed wingchairs angled toward the fire made a comfortable conversation area. A cherry butler table nestled between the chairs close with a delicate china tea service atop. A floral area rug covered most of the cottage's stone floor bringing with it a coziness she didn't expect in this unknown world.

Maja filled a metal kettle and swung it over the flames before she settled into a wing chair. "It will be a while before the water is ready. Have a seat."

Why didn't the woman just blink them some tea? Taking the proffered seat, Stella folded her hands in her lap with her dirty bare feet crossed at the ankles and bent at a demure angle pretending she would be having tea with the Queen of England.

"Queen of England, ha." Maja chuckled, her eyes danced as she regarded Stella. "Got a few years on the gal. Let's talk about your world."

What world? "You mean the one I just left?" Who knew she had to differentiate between worlds. The cat jumped into her lap and kneaded her thighs, before lying down.

"Calisto likes you. High approval. He doesn't like many." The kettle gurgled and hissed over the fire. Maja used a metal poker and hooked the metal arm that suspended the kettle and swung it off the fire. Her fingers wrapped around the hot metal handle without demonstrating any discomfort, while she talked as she poured a steamy plume of water into the china pot. *"Your world, the one we're in right now. Your thoughts created it."*

Nothing made sense. The drugs and alcohol must have colored her perceptions. Her right hand played with a tendril of hair, bringing it to her mouth to chew on, a nervous habit from her childhood. What if Maja was right? She couldn't be. *"No offense, but I couldn't have made this world. I don't know about you so how could I imagine you."*

The woman hooked the empty kettle back on the arm. She placed the tiny china lid on the pot before she heaved a dramatic sigh and fell back in her chair with both hands crossed over her heart. *"Don't remember me. My heart is breaking."*

"Oh, oh, I'm sorry. I do remember you. I just misspoke." Her initial urge was to comfort the woman, but Calisto's presence on her lap kept her seated. *"I mean you're very important, and I. Ah,"* she stammered to a stop unaware of the proper protocol for when you insulted a Goddess or a demi-goddess, not that she'd had a conversation with any before.

"Be at peace, child. I know you don't know me. I inserted myself in your world because I thought you needed guidance to get where you need to go, to live the life you were destined to live." Maja reached forward covering Stella's hand resting on Calisto's back.

A wave of serenity swept through Stella, pushing out her anxiety, fears, and failures as it moved through her. Warmth wrapped around her as she relaxed in the chair listening to the low-throated purr of the contented cat.

"That's why I don't blink up a cup of tea like your television witches and divine entities do. I choose to save my power for the important things. Let's get to work."

Get to work. The words implied she needed to do something. She exhaled slowly balanced on a euphoric high. Her head rolled back on the chair, her face upward. Across the ceiling marched numerous monsters and imps with sly eyes and expectant faces. Their glowing eyes fixed on her waiting for her next breath, next step, or more likely her next stumble. Then they would descend on her, ripping her apart with their wicked claws and sharp teeth. A shudder shivered through her body as the warmth disappeared.

Maja removed her hand and scooted back in her chair. "Sorry, dear, but too much euphoria just leaves you floating around in the clouds and good for nothing."

Wiggling her hips, Stella slid down in the chair, without disturbing the cat, and lengthened the space between herself and the waiting creatures. How could Maja endure living with so many ominous creatures?

"Tea's done." Maja poured the tea into the cups with a dramatic flourish, which demonstrated years of experience. "One lump or two."

"Three." Stella croaked the words. Who cared if sugar rotted her teeth, padded her waistline, and caused premature wrinkles

when demons hovered above? It'd be hard accepting a cup from her awkward position, but if she straightened up, she'd be closer to the fiends.

A plump scaly creature with tiny wings fluttered down from the ceiling, landing on the top of her wing chair. His shadow enveloped her, as did his sulfuric brimstone breath as his lips parted revealing sharp, yellow canines. As their eyes met, she drew up her legs to make herself as small as possible. Calisto bounded off her lap with a plaintive meow.

"Banish your self-doubt the way you did that Cam fellow," Maja ordered as she calmly stirred her tea.

Inhaling deeply, Stella's tight embrace of her arms loosened, allowing her hands to drop into her lap. She broke eye contact and brought her hands together in a light slap. "Be gone," she whispered. The shadow remained, along with the bad breath.

The sound of a heavy sigh filled the room. Maja placed her cup of tea back on the table. "Like you mean it." She clapped her hands together, sounding like thunder. "Desist, cease, halt, and flee from me now, I say." Her powerful voice filling the cottage caused the fire to leap. The shadow vanished.

Stella sat up in her chair. "Thanks. Appreciate it." An upward glance revealed plenty of monsters waiting, but their sense of gloating vanished along with a few of their brethren. Maja packed a punch.

"Oh dear, I only wanted to demonstrate. You have the strength if you only believe in yourself. You're so incredibly capable. In time, you'll be a guide." Her fingers lifted a delicate cup brimming with tea and offered it to Stella.

"Thanks." The fragrant steaming cup added normalcy to a scene that was anything but. "How can I be a guide? Do I guide souls through the dark forest?"

Maja sipped her tea with enjoyment as her eyes rolled upward. "Hmm, nothing a good cup of tea can't make better. My own blend by the way." She took another sip, held it in her mouth, before swallowing.

Stella emulated her host's behavior by bringing the teacup to her lips. The aromatic fragrance wafted on the air as she tried to place the spices. Ginger, cardamom, cinnamon, a citrusy tang, and a hint of something else she couldn't name wove together in a harmonious dance. The warm, sweet liquid flowed over her tongue, awakening the taste buds and leaving them bereft when she swallowed. The former feeling of comfort that had so rudely left her returned.

"This tea is magic."

Her host nodded in agreement before putting her cup down. "Some say that, but the intentions I endow it with is the real magick. Remember how you felt when Cam appeared, annoying you with his self-absorbed, critical chatter."

Her timber tentative, Stella replied, "Yes." Odd that Maja knew Cam's name but maybe it came with the territory, or she'd plucked it from her mind.

"Go back and examine your emotions. Describe them to me."

A moment that happened, less than twenty minutes ago, was already fading as she tugged at the threads to weave it back together. "I was..." she hesitated, reaching for the right descrip-

tion, "upset."

"Upset? That's what happens when two seeds fall into one hole, instead of one when I'm gardening. Were you only upset?" She probed gently, inflaming the sore spot Stella had already rubbed raw.

"No!" She jerked forward sloshing the tea over the rim of her cup. To avoid any more accidents, she placed the cup back on the table and stood. The emotions came pouring back, unsettling her with their impact and setting her in motion. Her pacing carried her across the width of the small cabin, giving her a chance to examine the tapestries in the shadows. One was a man bear or a bear-man.

Her attention jerked back to her anger at Cam. Her fingers closed into fists as she uttered a small growl. "Cam is the problem. The reason I'm here." Stopping, she stomped one foot, forgetting stone lay underneath the carpet. "I couldn't stand seeing his smug face, always critical, telling me what I should do, and pushing me. I'd had enough, couldn't stand the sight of him or his pompous attitude. I wanted both of them gone." She slammed her hands together as she growled the last word.

A few of the creatures hanging from the ceiling winked out of existence. Did she do that?

"Ah, such skill, such potential. I'm impressed in such a young mortal. There's a reason I chose you."

"You chose me?" The thought astounded her. All her life she'd worked hard to be good enough. Even if it was kickball or math bowl, she never wanted to be the person who sucked, the one who caused her team to lose. Playing it safe guaranteed she *wouldn't make costly mistakes or huge triumphs either. Never the rabbit, always the tortoise. Why a deity would choose her baffled her. "Why?"*

Maja rubbed a jewel-bedecked long-fingered hand over her face. "I see some of my younger self in you. Not enough confidence in your natural abilities. Our world is several layers thick with entities existing in each realm. Occasionally, the domains overlap, and you spy someone or something from another realm. It could be a glimpse of the future, someone from the past, a voice, a suggestion whispered just when you needed it. Has that ever happened to you?"

"More than once." She never told anyone, certain she was losing her mind. It would be enough for her mother to insist on an exorcism.

"Can you describe this experience?" Maja encouraged as she leaned forward in her chair.

Everything blurred together, making it hard to pick out individual experiences. Her breathing became frantic as she searched her mind for details, only finding mists similar to what she encountered in the dark forest. "I can't remember. Everything is getting foggy. Is it my time to pass over?"

Maja stood and wrapped an arm around Stella, tucking her close. "Listen, child, our time is short. Your job involves finding your own answers and not be influenced by outside forces. You're not crossing over. You'll go back to the life you left. You're not dead."

"Not dead," she repeated the words trying to take them in. Just about the time she accepted being dead, she found out she

wasn't. "What happened?"

"You're in a comatose state due to the drugs, alcohol, and the desire not to live. Your body still lives, but your mind, along with your spirit, went on a voyage for answers," she murmured the words close to Stella's ear.

Did she find all the answers? Her death did no good. Excellent, since she wasn't dead. Cam would be a toothless threat if she alerted administration that he was threatening her, but first she needed to talk to Mitch. What seemed so hopeless didn't seem as bad now. As for her mother, she could accept she was similar to so many other people desperately searching for value and hope in all the wrong places. If only her mother found that younger, happier self. "I'm not ready. I need to know more."

Maja's other arm wrapped around her, pulling her into a tight hug. "Don't worry. I have a mentor for you. You'll recognize her when you meet her."

CHAPTER TWELVE

OW WILL I recognize her, she wanted to ask, but a gut-wrenching pain doubled her over. Eyes closed, breath held, she rode out the spasm. She heard voices, an argument. Her mother's voice rang out over the man's.

"My daughter needs medical help now."

Mom. Her eyes wouldn't open. Her lashes were tangled and caked together with what her mother used to call sandman's sand, but she only labeled gunk. The high wail of a police car siren came closer and then stuttered to a stop. Someone bumped into her bed frame, jostling her, causing the rope to rub on her wrists. Great Goddess, they'd tied her up. Nausea that threatened before returned, causing a thin spray of vomit. Basic first aid knowledge had her turning her head to prevent it from sliding back down her throat.

"Stay if you want, Roberta, but I'm not getting arrested."

People ran by her, and a door slammed.

The mattress depressed as her mother sat beside her legs. "I'm not leaving my daughter."

A fierce pounding rattled the door. "Police. Open up."

The mattress creaked as Roberta stood, crossed the room, and opened the door. "Thank goodness, you got here. That horrible man and his thugs just ran out the back door. They tortured my daughter because of her religion. Forced me to watch. A regular hate crime."

Stella listened to her mother as she broke down in tears, confessing her love for her daughter and her stupidity in trusting the snake oil salesman posing as a holy messenger. Disgust, hate, even contempt should have overwhelmed Stella, but she kept listening for even a hint of Bobby, and then she heard it.

"I should have known the man was no good. He didn't even believe in musical instruments."

Someone sawed diligently away at her restraints. "Don't worry. We'll get this off of you." Her right arm came free, leaving behind a deep ache in her shoulder blade. Rolling it eased the stiffness a little.

"She's conscious," a female voice exclaimed. "We need water to wash her face."

A cool damp towel covered her eyes, wiping away the gunk. Finally, she could open her eyes. The anxious face of her mother filled her vision. "Can you ever forgive me?"

After kidnapping and possible exorcism, theirs would never be a television family relationship. Still, she could forgive her mother and move on. "It's okay, Bobby. Everyone goes down a wrong path now and then, trusting people who don't deserve their respect, let alone trust."

Her mother's eyes grew wide as she stepped back.

"I think you need some water." The female officer brandished a bottle, propped her up, and dribbled the water down her throat. It felt good, relieving the dryness, but not quite up to the delicious hot tea, Maja brewed. Had she imagined it all? Some crazy dream brought on by too many painkillers.

The rope snapped off her left leg as an officer sawed through it with a lethal-looking blade. She wiggled her feet, lifting up her rear from the mattress, testing to see if her leg still functioned. It still worked, but it hurt. The rope restraint around her right ankle dropped to the floor as a pair of medics rushed into the room with a gurney.

A medic knelt down beside the bed and donned latex gloves. "I'm Sean. I'll be examining you to make sure nothing is broken before we put you on the gurney."

Stella nodded her head unsure if she were supposed to introduce herself at this point. Who knew how long she'd been tied to the bed? Her rank body odor wrinkled her nose and partially answered her question. Sean gently picked up her arms, examining them. "Several long scratches, the type you'd expect from briars."

"What? Let me see?" Her mother, trying to look around the medic, resisted her involuntary escorting out by an officer, and stared back as she left.

Sean continued his survey as the other medic made notes. "I'm going to roll you on your side to check your spine before lifting."

The other medic assisted in rolling her carefully onto her side, pressing her abused shoulder into the mattress. A small groan escaped as she surveyed the room, though it was a little hard to see between all the uniformed legs. The walls were dirty, with holes in the drywall a little larger than a closed fist. A card table with an oversized Bible and a wooden cross on top of it reminded her of one of the scenes from a vampire movie she'd watched. Abandoned metal chairs lying on the floor bore witness to the speed of the escape.

"Her legs are filthy, covered in dirt." The medic commented while a large flash went off. A scraping sound along with pressure on her left shin alerted her to an officer scraping dried mud into a plastic evidence bag. Scratches, dust, knowledge, it all had to be real. The Pleiades, the Seven Sisters, she'd have to look those up.

"I need to see her! Please."

Mitch's voice had her twisting around to catch sight of his face. He stood in the door flanked by two officers. His tight lips expressed a determination she knew well.

"This is a crime scene. You could contaminate it." One officer explained, blocking Mitch's entrance by positioning himself in the middle of the open doorway.

Mitch held his ground. He must have called the police. Of course, he did. Despite all her mother's protestations to the authorities and fast forming regret, she might not have made it if not for Mitch.

"I'm okay. Meet me at the hospital," she told him.

"Which one?" His voice carried over the noise of the various individuals collecting evidence.

A medic answered for her, which was just as well since she had no clue where she was going. The two medics lifted and covered her with a blanket before strapping her in. The material, tucked tight around her toes all the way up her body, warmed her. The gurney clicked in place as they raised it and maneuvered it through the cramped fetid room.

Slanting sun cut through the bare tree branches as the medics backed out of the building. Strapped down, her vision was limited to blue sky with the occasional wispy cloud and bare tree branches. The crisp air carried a hint of burning in it. Nice to be outside. Alive.

Mitch's tall figure caught her eye. He waved, giving her a cautious smile, his worry reflected in the position of his hunched shoulders.

A small dark woman rushed forward and stuck a mike in her face. "Is it true you were the intended sacrifice in a Satanic ritual?"

Seriously? She wished they'd put the blanket over her head. Sean, the medic closest to the reporter yelled, "Get out of the way. You're compromising her medical care."

Mitch joined in, moving his tall form between the gurney and the reporter as the medics wheeled the gurney to the waiting ambulance. The reporter was part of the problem. Time to make a stand. "Mitch," she pushed the words past dry lips. "Tell the reporter I was not a satanic ritual sacrifice. Satanists do not sacrifice people or animals. That's all movie nonsense."

His somber eyes held hers as he nodded. "I'll tell them, but I don't know if it will do any good. The news is all about sensationalism and preying on people's secret fears. Reporters don't care about the truth."

"Thank you."

The female medic spoke to Mitch, "You're done. We've got to get your girlfriend to the hospital."

"Yes." He never bothered to correct the term, girlfriend.

Then again, it wasn't like him to confide in a random uni-formed stranger. *Oh, we just work together and occasionally share secret chunks of our lives. I would like her to be my girlfriend, but she brushes off my overtures to chase after some hot bad boy.*

Good thing he never mentioned it. In the end, it made her sound stupid, probably because she had been. Not anymore. The gurney snapped in place inside the ambulance while Sean attached a blood pressure device to monitor her pulse.

The female medic took her temperature while she chatted. "My name is Jill. Your boyfriend is a good one. He protected you from the reporters and knew exactly what you needed to have done."

"He did, didn't he?" She never really thought about it, but Mitch always seemed to know what she needed. Why hadn't she ever realized how attuned the two of them were. Too busy meeting Cam's various needs—make that demands.

Jill typed some info into a small mounted computer. "Yeah, it's hard to find a man who will treat a girl well."

Sean rolled his eyes and reached for the grab rod. "Jill, you better hold on and talk less."

The woman followed his advice but merely grunted in response to his comment. The ambulance's wail was intensely loud inside the compartment. The vehicle weaved in and out of traffic and occasionally gave a stronger blast. Despite the straps, Stella felt the sway of the gurney, but at least she wasn't jerked around as much as Jill and Sean. They reminded her of human laundry on a metal clothesline in the middle of a tornado. Only the tightly packed ambulance kept them from flying away.

"We're here," Sean announced as the ambulance slowed and bumped up into the driveway. The doors swung open and hands reached out to guide the gurney down. Questions flew.

"Blood loss?"

"Heart Rate?"

"Pressure?"

What she could gather from the comments was she suffered dehydration, shock, trauma to the joints from being tied, lacerations, and abrasions. No mention of her filthy feet.

Some of the people waiting looked up at her entrance, possibly cursing her arrival because it would mean an added delay until their exam. Another news reporter milling in the crowded lobby spotted her and made a break for the gurney. No Mitch was there to run interference although someone shouted for security.

Interference came in the form of Esmeralda Hare brandishing her wolf-headed cane. "Stand back or I'll turn you into a toad."

The male reporter stumbled backward. The cane, the threat, or Esmeralda's sudden appearance may have contributed to his reaction. Could it have been something else? Like Maja watching over her? Who knew? She did know the things weren't always, as they seemed. Even when she thought she was alone and friendless, forces she didn't understand were beside her.

Hospital personnel surrounded her and lifted her from one gurney to another. "Good luck, kid," Jill wished her before letting go of the gurney.

After being looked over by a half-dozen people with various titles, Stella made it upstairs to a private room. An IV rehydrated her while a monitor beeped in the background assuring everyone she was okay. The nurse checked her pulse, wrote it down and gave her a weary smile. "I imagine you left a nightmare. Scary" The woman shivered for effect. "Nothing a couple of days of forced rest and being pampered by your family won't fix."

Of course, that would require a family who would do that. A little sigh caught in her throat as her father walked through the door looking haggard and much older than she remembered. He bent over and kissed her forehead before dropping into a nearby chair. "How's my best girl?"

The childhood nickname made her heart trip. What she would have given for such a casual endearment even a couple of weeks ago. That time was gone. "They tell me I'm alive. Good considering I was unconscious for thirty-six hours without food or water. Where's Mother?"

"Umm, she had some paperwork to finish with the police." Her father stared down at his shoes. Under arrest was what he didn't say. Just as well, she didn't want to see her anytime soon.

Her father brushed his hand against hers. "Pamela thought maybe you could spend a couple of days with us."

Geesh. She fought hard not to roll her eyes. His new, much younger wife gave him official permission to allow his recently kidnapped and abused daughter to come home with him. What an invite. She hoped to avoid the dubious charms of Pammy but wasn't sure what other options she had. She'd turn down her mother if she weren't in jail. "Oh, I don't know. How about I get back to you."

A commotion near the door revealed Mitch, Leah, and the entire Carpenter family crowding the entrance. Her father picked up her hand and kissed it. "I understand. I'll get out of here so you can see the people you want to see."

"No, you don't have to go."

His shoulders pitched forward as he left without replying. He looked pathetic. A voice that sounded remarkably like Maja's spoke. "Don't feel too sorry for him. He made his choices and left a wave of devastation behind. It's his mess if he wants to clean it up."

So true. It was hard to think of her parents screwing up, but they did, making them seem a lot more human and not the least bit god-like. The Carpenters along with Mitch spilled into the room. The usually reticent Mitch made sure to take the only chair in the room, pulling it close to the bed.

"I apologize if I'm embarrassing you, but I figured I needed to get to the front of the boyfriend line with Cam being in jail and all." Mitch reached through the bed railing to rest his hand on hers. "Do I get to the front of the line? My heart stopped when I realized something happened to you?"

A few "ahs" came from Leah and Nora. Esmeralda grumbled, "Get on with it. We got important stuff too."

Feeling suddenly better, she turned her hand to grip Mitch's. "You're already at the front. You always should have been."

Mitch's eyes brightened along with his expression. Pure joy illuminated his face. How could she have ever thought Cam cared about her? He never looked at her the way Mitch did.

"No, no, no," Esmeralda shook her head as she walked toward the bed. "Make the man work, grovel, and keep him uncertain. Make him dance. Don't tell him he's number one. Sheesh, girls today." The rest of the family laughed.

Mitch mouthed, *Thank you,* and topped it off with a wink.

Leah and Nora crowded the left side of her bed while Mitch relinquished his chair to Esmeralda, earning him a promise not to turn him into a toad.

"Nana," Leah added, "quit threatening to turn people into toads. You know you can't do that."

Instead of Esmeralda answering, her dapper husband Buell stepped forward attired in a double-breasted suit and tie. "I wouldn't bet on that. The woman can do anything she sets out to do. I wanted to hear more about this Cam character who sounds toad worthy."

"Me, too," Stella added, wondering if she had anything to fear from Cam. Mitch stepped closer to the group as he explained.

"Initially, I alerted everyone about your absence. I contacted campus security who went to your room. Cece, your roommate, swore Cam killed you and that she saw him and some other guys carrying you out and everything."

"That wasn't Cam." She interrupted the story, trying to put the pieces together. "Cece was probably high when she came back." No other reason in explaining why she'd connect Cam with the hired muscle and the black SUV.

"Yeah, we know that now," Leah, commented. She circled her hand. "C'mon finish the story. I never heard all of it. Just bits and pieces."

Mitch nodded, but his gaze went to Stella. "Is me talking about it bothering you?"

"No! Please tell. How else will I know?" She didn't feel the need to explain she'd washed down a handful of drugs with alcohol. Later, with a smaller group, although, according to Leah, more than half of her family had the ability to have already sensed it.

Mitch brushed her hair back as she leaned into his touch. Esmeralda cleared her throat, which started Mitch talking. "Cece rattled off Cam's address like she'd memorized it or something. Police went over there. No response. They broke in due to having probable cause. Boxed up DVD players, laptops, and game systems crowding the small apartment, but no Cam, and no Stella. They had to send a van for the stolen merchandise."

Ethan elbowed his way to the front of the group. "How did they know it was stolen? Could be the guy had a lot of stuff."

"Well, apparently some electronics store had been broken into earlier, and the items matched the description of what was stolen."

Did Cam burglarize the electronics store? If you'd asked her last week, she'd have defended him. So much, she didn't know about Cam. Bizarre, she'd known him for weeks and knew almost zilch. All she knew was that he excelled at manipulating women.

Nora scratched her head, considering the details. "Where was Cam when this happened?"

Mitch held up one finger. "Now, that's where it gets peculiar. He was busy breaking into the computer lab. In fact, he was in the lab and had a computer powered up, but couldn't get past the password. He had no clue the door was alarmed. When caught, he insisted Stella gave him permission to be there. The campus police had him in the car when the county police zoomed up and grabbed him. The truth is he didn't kidnap you or murder you, but he either robbed the store or accepted stolen merchandise, and did break into the computer lab. If that wasn't enough, he swung at one of the arresting officers."

"Out of curiosity, were the officers all men?" Stella asked, wondering if uniformed women would be able to withstand his legendary skills.

Mitch shot her an interested look, hoisting one eyebrow. "I don't know."

Leah pointed to Stella. "How did you find out where she was?"

"Ah, that. You're the only one who's asked. The police just took the address and went with it." Mitch ran a hand through his thick hair. "I remembered Stella saying something about her mom attending The Last Days and Holy Resurrection Tabernacle or something like that. Not too many churches named that in her town, two to be exact."

He stopped talking with two bright spots of red on his cheeks. Stella told him, "It doesn't matter what you did. The results are the only thing that matter. Okay?"

"Um, right." He managed a smile and then shrugged. "At the first church, I got a disconnected message. I called the second church. Whoever answered the phone informed me that both Roberta and the minister left to look at church property. It was some big deal because they took some other investors with them, even rented a black Escalade to view the property. She saw it when she came into work. I confessed I was one of the big investors and wanted to catch up with them. Did she know where they went? Somewhere around the college, and then she made a remark about the license on the rental being funny. I asked why. It read STD 234, which made it an easy one to remember."

"Very convenient," Maura, Leah's mother, commented working her way up from the back of the crowd to stand near the bed. She reached over the footboard to pat Stella's feet. "After you get out of the hospital, you're coming home with us. With Nora gone, there's a room practically with your name on it."

At last, a solution to her home problem offered in a casual invite "Yes, I'd like that."

Ethan interrupted, "Everyone knows we're taking Stella home with us. It goes without saying." He sauntered up to Mitch and elbowed him. "The story, man."

"I used a realty site to look for isolated properties, not close to anything. Something preferably abandoned, so there'd be no real interest in it and found about four probable places. My plan was to casually survey the sites, but my lack of wheels slowed down the process. It's hard to convince a friend to drive you to abandoned buildings. I tried using one of those online sites that supposedly helps you find information for a fee. Worthless. By this time, I knew Stella had been gone over twenty-four hours. I was getting desperate and hacked into the tax assessor's website. Not that hard, really. I found out the addresses for derelict buildings. Out of state owners held the first two buildings. The Last Days and Holy Resurrection Tabernacle owned the third. Bingo. I called the police and explained I was a friend of Stella's and had reason to believe she was being held against her will at that location. I had to get a taxi to take me out to the middle of nowhere, which is rather hard to convince a taxi driver to do when he's worried you'll rob him."

Stella rubbed Mitch's hand against her face. "How could someone not trust you? You don't have a criminal bone in your body."

Mitch's face erupted into a goofy, so in love smile, the rest of the group elbowed one another. "If you don't count lying and hacking into databases."

"Let's go get something to eat," Maura suggested, catching everyone's eye as she left the room.

Ethan was the last to go. "I hope you know that's code for giving you two time alone. Use it well."

Stella's grip tightened on Mitch's hand. "I need to talk to you." She didn't want to mention it when everything appeared to be working out, but she still needed to.

Mitch reached for her other hand. "Go ahead, sweetheart. You can tell me anything."

The look in his eyes reassured her. "Cam blackmailed me. He threatened to get you in trouble because he found out about your DUI."

"Is that why you went out with him?" Mitch looked both concerned and confused as he played with her hand, using his index finger to outline her fingers and sending a jolt of electricity up her arm.

"Hmm." His actions made her forget the question for a second. "No, I went out because he kept asking me."

"That's all it took, huh?" Mitch continued to play with her hand not looking up. "If I'd known that then I would have taken that approach."

"Wish you had." Stella didn't add they could have avoided this entire mess, but maybe they wouldn't have. Her mother still would have kidnapped her. Only she may not have been out of it as much. They used drugs on her, too, ether or chloroform so it may not have made much of a difference.

Mitch's eyebrows lowered as his lips turned down. It didn't take clairvoyance to realize he blamed himself. "We could have had so much more time together watching movies, holding hands, eating pizza, and snuggling."

"Snuggling, I'm all for that."

He looked up and grinned, the worry gone from his eyes. She hated to put it back, but she wanted to have an honest relationship. "He wanted me to change grades on the computer, his and six friends. I think he was close to being kicked out for academic failure and probably taking money from the others."

Mitch snorted. "Yeah, I hear you actually have to show up in class to pass."

"Well, apparently Cam didn't hear it, and he failed to meet the right girls to do his homework. Kept getting dumb ones."

"You're smart. I know that. I had a peek at your grades. You're setting the curve in some of your classes."

Stella grinned. "Thanks." She threw him a significant look. "You'll lose your job if you get caught accessing privileged files."

"I did it from Lauren's computer."

They both laughed.

"What I have to tell you I'm not proud of. I took a bunch of pills and washed them down with vodka. I felt there was no way out. If I didn't do what Cam wanted, you'd have lost your scholarship."

"Stella," Mitch leaned over the railing gathering her in his arms, careful of the IV. "Screw the scholarship. You're all I care about. Besides, a failing student and felon isn't exactly Mr. Credible. I'm so sorry you didn't tell me. Remember you can tell me anything, no matter what."

She sniffed. "Okay, I'm a practicing Wiccan too."

"Oh that, you told me that before."

"I did?" She didn't remember doing that. "When?"

"Oh, never directly, but you always were the go-to person about any earth-based religion. I figured it out. I'm smart like that."

"On that note," Esmeralda trilled from the doorway. "I have someone I want you to meet."

A tall woman stood behind the diminutive Nana. The woman followed Esmeralda slowly, using a cane. A gray braid trailed down her back.

"Maja." The name escaped Stella's lips.

Esmeralda looked truly taken back. "You know Mary? Only her friends call her Maja."

"You could say we met in another place, another dimension."

A look of comprehension settled over Esmeralda. "Then you know why she's here. Don't you?"

Mitch looked from woman to woman. "I don't. Why?"

Stella's eyes teared up a little. "She's to be my teacher, mother, and grandmother."

Maja grinned. "I told you that you'd recognize your mentor when you met her. The teacher arrives when the student is ready."

THE END

Like this book? Read the entire series. Find out more at www.raynanoire.com.

Book One

Pagan Eyes: Initiation

Book Two

Pagan Eyes: Revelation

Book Three

Pagan Eyes: Declaration

INITIATION

Pagan Eyes, Book 1

BY

Rayna Noire

NANA HOBBLED INTO the living room, dragging her left leg behind her, waving the evening newspaper. Red-faced and out of breath, she drew everyone's attention. Mother ran over to her, wrapping one arm around her and urging her to sit down.

"Please, Mama, you must calm down. It's not good for your heart."

Father nodded from his place in the kitchen doorway, drying a plate. Leah's brother, Ethan, watched his grandmother with an expectant expression and drawn breath, probably certain she'd fall to the floor, as she had only a couple of months before. Luckily, they all lived together. She'd never have survived the stroke on her own. The doctor had instructed them to keep her calm, but often Nana demonstrated the high drama associated with a teenage girl.

Leah stood up and walked over to her grandmother, taking the newspaper from her hand. "What is it, Nana?"

Her brother announced from his spot on the couch, "It's the cyber-bullying article on the front page. I've no worries, Nana. No one bullies me." Ethan pushed up his sleeve and clenched his fist to display a meager bicep, though probably more than most ten-year-olds could lay claim to.

A smile crossed the woman's lined face. "No, sweetheart, no, this is much worse."

Leah's mother, Maura, managed to get Nana to sit in a chair with some difficulty, since only one leg worked right. Leah looked away. It reminded her of the time she'd watched a three-legged dog lie down. The dog never acted like it minded, but it still made her feel bad watching it.

Crouching beside the chair, her mother took Nana's hand. "Tell me, tell us."

Pointing with one hand to Leah, who still clutched the newspaper, she commanded, "Read it to them. Let them know the barbarians still exist. There is no justice, no fairness, no equal rights, and no protection." Her voice became louder and stronger with each word. Her body shook as she half rose from the chair.

Mother cut her eyes meaningfully at her husband, who nodded at Leah, who paged through the paper.

Leah searched for what could be upsetting her grandmother. "Lead story is local boy signing with an NFL contract." Both her father and mother shook their heads no. She kept paging through the paper. "A huge storm is predicted for the Northeast?"

Grandmother waved her hand in a circle to keep going.

"Ah." She knew that wasn't the right story, but what could it be? On the back page of the front section near the fold was a small article. She knew instinctively it was the one her grandmother meant. "Yesterday, in Papua, New Guinea, a twenty-year-old woman accused of being a witch was burned alive. The young widow and mother left two small children behind."

Her grandmother shook off her daughter's hand. Stabbing

the air with an emphatic index finger, she crowed, "See? See? They're at it again." Her dark eyes darted around the room to make sure she had everyone's attention. "That poor girl. What was her crime, really?"

Maura sighed. "Just twenty, so young. Could be she was too pretty and attracted a married man's eye. Calling her a witch is always a good way to get rid of her. It worked countless times before."

Her father laid down the plate and towel and walked into the living room to join the conversation. He sat down on the couch on the other side of Ethan. "Something happened in their village. Chickens weren't laying or a goat died. It's always easier to blame it on the evil eye or a hex, than accept it for what it is. Just life, luck, usually both. People always seem to believe life owes them more than they deserve. The only way to rationalize not getting it is to blame someone for blocking it."

Ethan joined in. "Just like calling someone a cheat, a liar, or even a bully."

"In a way," Maura agreed. "But not exactly. People don't feel it is okay to kill people for telling a lie or even being accused of telling a lie. The hatred goes bone deep, associated with fear and helplessness. Even the simple fact she had no man to stand for her would be enough to persecute her."

Leah stood, silent, thinking that only a few years separated her from the young woman burned alive. Yesterday, her history teacher, Miss Santiago, had grown as animated as Nana talking about human slavery in the US. Her voice had become shrill as she'd spoken of undocumented workers not receiving any pay for their work and being kept in unheated garages, treated no better than animals. After class, the popular girls, Lauren, Brianna, and Alexis, had joked about Miss Santiago's behavior, even pretending to be her, waving their arms and bugging out their eyes, spitting out the words. Most of the other students had pretended to enjoy their performance. Leah hadn't. Besides being mean, she'd had no reason to appease the girls. She already knew she was on their short list.

Yeah, she knew her teacher had gone overboard, but she knew without having it spelled out that it was personal. Often Leah knew things without words, just as she knew someone close to Miss Santiago had died under such conditions. Leah knew all about taking things personally. A woman burned as a witch was personal for her family. How could it not be when her entire family followed the old ways?

Her family circled her grandmother, trying to calm her down without much success. Leah leaned back against the wall the offending newspaper still in her hand, she wanted to throw it to the ground and flee. An image took shape in her mind. It was dark, most likely night. The sound of running, yelling, and then screaming, a long prolonged scream as if whoever uttered it felt absolute terror. A spark charged the night, then caught fire and became a flame, growing into an orb of light. It illuminated sweaty, dark faces with feverish eyes and determined countenances. Two strong men stripped to the waist held a woman between them. Her long hair covered her face as she struggled.

Off to the side, a chair sat on a dais. An almost skeletal

man sat there, garbed in a long robe. His lips quirked up as the men wrestled the woman, who wore a coarse, shapeless gown, to a standstill in front of him. A brutal push shoved her to her knees. The sound of weeping almost broke Leah's heart. She was watching what had happened in New Guinea only days before.

No doubt, the man on the dais had caused this woman to be in such a situation. The crying continued as the man ordered. "Let me look on the face of the witch." The surrounding crowd hissed and murmured. Most threw their hands in front of their faces or looked away as if looking at the woman's face might cause harm. She couldn't. The woman deserved her respect. One guard grabbed her long dark hair and yanked, snapping her head up. Despite the tears glistening on her skin, her expression was defiant. Her face was familiar. It should have been, since she saw it every morning in the mirror as she brushed her hair.

Her legs, more rubberlike than bone and muscle, slid out from under her, landing her on the floor. What did it mean? Nana used to tell her the visions she received were similar to a tornado watch. It didn't necessarily mean the vision would happen, but it was best to get ready for it in case it did. Most of her visions included small things, such as being ridiculed by Lauren and Brianna or failing an algebra test, or slipping on the ice and losing two teeth. It all had happened, except the teeth. Whenever she saw anything glistening like ice, she avoided it, keeping her teeth intact so far.

The image of the man on the dais chilled her, unlike any amount of teeth-cracking ice could. The clothes she wore, the way the man spoke, none of it made sense. Her mother's voice broke into her daze.

"Leah, what are you doing? Try to be of some help, will you? Go get your grandmother a glass of water. Ethan, go get Nana's protection heart charm from the box in her bedroom."

Pushing up to her knees, she watched her brother scamper out of the room to retrieve the charm. Her mother threw her an irritated look, probably because she was still sitting there. Standing, she walked to the kitchen, but she could hear them talking. Her grandmother's shrill voice carried.

"Maura." Her voice had an imperious tone that defied her fragile appearance. "Be gentle with your daughter. Soon, she will be called on to make the ultimate sacrifice."

The ultimate sacrifice? The water splashed over the glass rim as she continued to hold it under the faucet, not seeing it but instead the glee in the man's face who'd called her a witch. She truly hoped her grandmother didn't expect her to become a burnt offering.

Turning off the faucet, she tipped the glass to pour out the excess water. Taking a dishtowel, she dried the glass. Nana could trace her ancestry back to Romany gypsies. She claimed this centuries-old bond allowed her to turn the Tarot cards with surprising accuracy for her loyal clients. Leah had doubts about her grandmother's actual ability, though the fact she'd seen the same clients faithfully for years made Leah wonder. Then there were the crystals and charms strewn about the family home, which kept her from inviting classmates over. All she really wanted was just to be another teenage girl obsessed with drama and boys. Well, only the boys part...one boy,

Dylan Torres, if she was honest with herself.

As she handed the glass to Nana, their hands touched. Her grandmother's eyes gleamed dark with intelligence. The brief glance conveyed awareness of Leah's inner turmoil and comfort. It was the equivalent of kneeling to bury her face against Nana's shoulder, sobbing out her confusion, her fears, and her inappropriate attraction to Dylan, whose father happened to be a Pentecostal minister. A bad thing about the Pentecosts was the fact they actually believed witches existed and shouldn't, rather like cockroaches.

As her grandmother's fingers touched hers, the look, the touch, and the sudden knowledge that her legacy was to never be a normal girl caused her heart to plummet. No matter what excuses she might make for Nana's uncanny ability, she recognized Nana was never wrong.

Curious why so many well-heeled ladies would come month after month to have her grandmother tell their fortunes, she'd asked. Nana's answer had implied that knowing helped people shape their destiny and relieved stress. Seeing herself about to be burned at the stake didn't make her feel less stressed. Rather, just the opposite.

✧ ✧ ✧ ✧

NANA EVENTUALLY CALMED down. Adam, Leah's father, talked his determined mother-in-law out of calling the news organizations. Any negative attention might influence her father's engineering job. Nana understood this on one hand, but on another, she didn't since she chose not to hide what she was. Her grandmother had as much bravado as a drag queen in full costume demonstrating for marriage equality. There was a good chance she was pecking out a letter to the editor on her old typewriter. Leah had noticed a few of the letters in the papers, signed as Pagan Philosopher, had sounded exactly like Nana in full rant.

Her father had never mentioned the letters, which meant he hadn't seen them or had realized he could exercise no control over his mother-in-law. For years, the family had maintained a careful balance trying to please both extended families. Father's family was ultra-religious and had named their children Adam and Eve, somehow missing the incestuous connotation in the pairing. Everything that was part of the secular world was not only evil, but also forbidden. How he and her mother had ended up together appeared to be an unfathomable question. It could have been the lure of the forbidden, but more likely, it had started out as lust. Her father never would put it so bluntly, but she had seen the pictures of them together in college. No doubt, many men had craved her mother's dark, almost foreign, beauty, but she'd chosen instead the shy, short, bespectacled engineering student.

Her mother's reasoning for their romance was he accepted her the way she was. It would be great if someone accepted Leah for who she was. She peered at her own image in the mirror, complete with a disbelieving smirk. It indicated her non-belief of her father's total acceptance of her mother. Nana had chided her son-in-law on numerous occasions for keeping quiet about their religious beliefs. Inquiries from his parents asking if they'd been to church that week were usually appeased by saying they had. He intentionally forgot to mention their services took place on a farm ten miles out of town, often under the light of a full moon. Her father had decided to follow the old ways to humor his wife, but Leah suspected it was mainly to get his mother-in-law off his back.

Setting her alarm clock for the school day, she noted five hours had passed since the news meltdown. Theodora, her cat, jumped on the bed, kneading the pillow with her paws as if preparing it. Leah knew the feline was making her own bed. Grabbing another pillow from the floor, she placed it on the bed. Dropping her clothes on the floor, she climbed between the cool sheets. Locking her hands behind her head, she stared at the ceiling, thinking about her parents' relationship. Her parents got along better than most. Her family life was unusual in that she had both original parents living in the same house. Still, she wanted more than what they had, something stronger, bolder, something void of the timidity her father demonstrated in hiding from his parents that Maura was a witch, as was her grandmother.

No doubt, they had figured out Esmeralda Hare was a bit different, loving to play up the image of the carnival fortune-teller with flowing skirts, too much jewelry, and always wishing everyone a blessed day or merry meet again. The word most commonly used for Nana was "colorful." Nora, Leah's older sister, had confided once she'd overheard an argument between their parents over her father never telling his parents they didn't celebrate Christmas or Easter. None of the kids had cared because they'd enjoyed the Easter baskets and Christmas presents given to them by their grandparents.

Grandfather had retired from the ministry the same time

his wife had divorced him. Instead of warning everyone to stay on the straight and narrow, he'd donned tie-dyed shirts, made home-brewed beer, and attended the concerts of aging rock stars. Nora had pointed out that Grandfather would accept the family's religion since he had changed so much on his own. Of course, her father chose to say nothing. As much as Leah loved her father, she acknowledged, if only to herself, most of his actions were motivated out of fear of being different or that people might not like him. It wasn't so much that he accepted mother just how she was, but rather she accepted him with his fears, worries, and rules, able to see past everything to the caring man inside.

Scratching Theodora's head, she confided to the cat, "I won't be like that. I am who I am. It doesn't matter what people think."

The feline blinked her eyes as if commenting on the bold statement. Leah sighed. "You're right. I know. For all my brave words, I am no better than my father." Balling up her fist, she pounded her pillow in disgust. "Coward, that's all I am."

Threading her fingers under Theo's heavy body, she cradled the cat. The cat let out a few plaintive mews, but resigned herself to the cuddling, even to the point of purring. "Theodora, what am I to do? I know I am a fraud. I talk of nothing of consequence to Dylan. Questions about homework, reactions to pop quizzes, and comments on the weather are another way to spell lame. Brianna, at least, flirts with him."

The popular blonde's flirtatious banter always seemed to switch on whenever she was near a cute guy. It didn't matter that her boyfriend, Marcus, was a senior football player who'd scored scholarships at six colleges. Could be Brianna was looking for a replacement, not that she'd consider Dylan. He was too small a deal for her, too young, not popular enough. His father was a minister, which made him the male equivalent to poison ivy. Brianna only flirted with him because Leah liked him. Worse, she'd confessed to liking Dylan in a brief spate of time when she and Brianna had been friends.

Looking back, she wondered if it had been some elaborate scheme to get information. No doubt, Brianna had relayed to Dylan that Leah had a serious crush on him. If it bothered him too much, he could stop talking to her. Then again, if he did like her, he could ask her out, which he hadn't. The third option was Brianna hadn't told him or he'd chosen not to believe her. If it were the last, then he'd showed more sense than Leah had.

"I can see your light on," her mother called through the locked door.

Leah clapped her hands, turning the light off. As a kid, she'd been so enamored of the clapper lamp that her parents had bought her one. Most people would label it hokey, but she still liked it.

"Good girl," her mother admonished, before tacking on, "Love you."

"Love you, too, Mom," she called back, closing her eyes, easing into sleep. Tomorrow would be another day, just like so many others. The image of the man in the throne-like chair flickered into being. Sitting up, she shook her head to shake the offending image out. "I refuse to dream about him. I'll think of something pleasant, such as Dylan asking me to the homecoming dance."

Lying back down, she let her eyelids flick closed. Maybe Dylan didn't dance. She'd heard some of those religions had rules against it. Something about if people danced, they'd end up having sex like rabbits. As she drifted off to sleep, her last thought was she couldn't remember ever seeing a dancing rabbit.

THE SMELL STRUCK her first. The acrid, smelly odor reminded her of her fourth-grade field trip to a pioneer village. The candle maker had intrigued her by dipping wicks in what she had assumed was wax until the woman explained it was made of animal fat from butchered animals. That's what it smelled like, along with the campfire aroma of burning wood.

In the misty night sky, a clouded crescent moon shed meager light on the surroundings. Turning slowly she examined the primitive thatched hut behind her. In the small front garden, a split log supported by two stumps served as a bench. An oaken bucket sat by a door that flew open. An elderly woman hobbled out, dressed in a black cloak. The woman reminded Leah of her grandmother, but instead of a look of fierce determination, terror pulled her face into an anxious mask. Reaching Leah, she tugged on her clothes, pushing her toward the woods. "Flee, flee, they come. Smell the torches." The woman pointed to a path winding toward the east.

A dim glow was coming from that direction, along with the sounds of voices and snapping branches as dozens of feet marched in their direction. An overwhelming desire to run after the unknown woman came over her. Another part of her wanted to see who was coming down the path. It was only a dream, right? People couldn't be hurt in a dream, or could they? She struggled to remember what her psychology teacher, Mr. Schaeffer, had said. He'd said either people couldn't be hurt by their fears or your fears could kill you by bringing on cardiac arrest.

A few men came into view, burly men garbed in shapeless garments, with wild hair and ragged beards, Held high, flickering torches illuminating a small circle around them. One held a curved knife, reminiscent of the scythe the grim reaper carried. It didn't bode well. One of the men spotted her, yelled, "Witch!" and charged her way. It was a definite bad sign, causing her to sprint toward the woods in the same direction as the old woman. Sticks, rocks, and briars pierced her feet, reminding her of her shoeless state. At home, she excelled in cross-country, but she had shoes, sunlight, and a feel for the course with no angry villagers behind her. The running men drew closer. Leah stumbled over a tree root, wasting precious time.

"Here, over here." The voice came from overhead. Staring up into the canopy of leaves, she saw a small hand motioning to her. Of course, hide in the trees. Why didn't she think of that? Grabbing the lowest limb, she pulled herself into the leafy covering. In the dark, she felt for the branches, climbing higher. Eventually she grabbed an ankle or calf, and received a hand up for her trouble, helping her climb higher.

Good Goddess, how many people were in this tree? She held her breath as the light and noise came closer. The few men below argued about which way to go, while a woman waded in with her opinion. "Samuel, let the witch get away. Mayhap he uses the witch for his own purposes."

One of the front-runners denied the accusations. "Martha seeks to harm my name, because I did not plight my troth with her."

The argument moved on a little farther away from the tree. Leah exhaled in a whoosh, thanking the stars for the scorned woman and lack of dogs. As if hearing her silent prayer, a long canine bay rent the air.

More footsteps ran underneath their tree, where there was some minor disagreement about which way to go, then they ran after the previous party. The sound of her heart was so loud in her ears she couldn't believe her pursuers hadn't heard it also. The barking dog came closer, along with the sound of its handler.

"Ar-roo, Ar-roo." The dog sounded close, very close. Its nails scratching at her tree stopped Leah's heart, or it felt like it. Stupid canine. She was history. She was ready to drop out of the tree and give herself up when a hand touched her and stopped her in the dark. A single word sounded in her ear. "Wait."

Two villagers stood under the tree, arguing. "Pull the hound off the tree. You will anger the tree spirits. Misfortune will befall us entering the forest at night."

"Umfrey, still your wild speech. You speak of the old ways. We are now all Christians by order of the king. Such talk will

cause the witch hunters to take you up."

"I tell you this, Collin. A decree does not make the tree spirits, the fairies, the mysterious lights in the woods cease to be. Do you think they bow to kings?"

The dog's protest about the lack of interest in his treed prey caused Leah's heart to slow a tiny bit, but not return to normal. Crouched in the tree, similar to blackbirds on the line, she waited with the still unseen others.

"Morn is coming, and the field needs plowing. Umfrey, I will return, not because of your fears of tree fairies and what not, but because I've land to attend to."

"Good call. Your Mary may have some porridge simmering over the fire."

She listened to them move away. The staying hand remained on her arm. They all crouched in the tree for what seemed like hours as they waited for each group of witch hunters to pass by them. Dawn colored the sky with a pink glow, giving way to the sun's rays.

Finally, the hand released Leah's arm. They dropped out of the tree, one by one, the old crone in the black cloak, a young woman a bit older than herself but not by much, and a man, which surprised her. "I didn't think they took men as witches." She covered her mouth with her hand, realizing she'd spoken the words aloud.

The young woman stared at her, "What manner of speech is this?"

Before she could answer, the weathered-looking man chose to answer her inquiry. "They take whoever has trespassed against the village elders in some form or manner. My sin is I accused the miller of using unfair scales. People like Old Margaret, who has no one to stand for her, also are taken."

Turning to the young woman, Leah touched her own chest with her hand. "My speech is different because I am from America."

"A Mer Rica." The young woman tried to sound out the name. "Strange, I never heard talk of such a place. My name is Sabina."

"Leah," she answered, pointing to herself.

Sabina cocked her head at her slightly, "Is that your real name or your witch name? It is best you do not speak your Christian name."

Her witch name? Her grandmother had insisted on giving her the witch name Raven, but she never used it. "I assume Sabina is your witch name."

Sabina bobbed her head as if the whole discussion was a no-brainer. "It is and isn't. I didn't have a witch name to begin with, but since we will go to a new town, I will need a new name. Sabina it is. Witches only give out their false name to each other else it will be spoken under the pain of torture."

It made sense. She remembered something about that when Nana had made her watch one of those online videos about the Burning Times, full of grainy black-and-white illustrations of people being tortured in myriad of ways. Guilty or innocent, somehow the people had always ended up dead.

Margaret started walking in the direction of her house. The man grabbed her arm. "No, someone will wait at the cottage for your return."

The old woman struggled in his grasp. "I must save Odo."

"Odo is a creature of the wild. He can take care of himself better than you," the man insisted, turning the woman to walk deeper into the woods.

A whoosh and the sound of crackling caused them all to turn in the direction of Old Margaret's house. A thick plume of smoke filled the air, darkening the morning sky. The old woman cried out, "That is all I have!" and shook in the man's half embrace.

Sabina stepped forward to touch the woman's cheek, wet with tears. "You have life, Margaret. Once the witch hunters come, you can never return home."

Sorrow swept over Leah for the weeping devastated woman weeping. Margaret raised her head to glare at Leah. Pulling herself out of comforting arms, she pointed one bony finger at Leah. "You are the reason they came. If I had not found you in the forest and took you and gave you succor, I would have my home and my beloved Odo."

Found her in the forest? At least that explained how she'd ended up here, but not really. "I am sorry. I did not mean to hurt you or Odo."

"Margaret," the man inserted. "You are speaking out of your loss. It was only a matter of time before they came for each of us. We all knew it. Why else did we create witch names or our dark clothing so we can vanish into the night? We do not call ourselves witches. We may not worship the new god or practice the old ways to ensure a good crop, but that does not make us

evil, or witches. Still, once others call us witches, we have to prepare."

Leah wanted to protest that witches weren't evil, but she listened and considered the trio. The man served as a sort of shepherd, as he managed to get everyone back on the trail through the woods. He nodded to Leah. "You can call me Henry."

Leah nodded to him, well aware that Henry probably wasn't his name. "Thanks. This is a new place for me, and I appreciate your help."

Henry nodded and gestured to the path ahead. "Make haste. Many have chores to do. Most fear the monks more who travel to villages stirring up suspicions with their talk of witches and intercourse with the devil. They will head back into the woods in search of people they can label witches. Their sins might have been lingering in the woods too long or picking herbs for a disorder instead of calling on a physician. I heard an entire town in Germany was taken up as witches, the children, and priests, too. The blood lust is on them, making me wonder if there will be any people left to populate the earth."

Leah shuddered. Hearing or reading about the Burning Times was something entirely different from walking through the woods with people accused of being witches. Not a good different, either. She preferred the distance accompanying a span of centuries. Still, there had to be a reason behind this. These dreams were more realistic than anything she had dreamt before. Was the universe speaking to her? Was this something she should understand? In a way similar to her father, she never *spoke about her faith. Could be she was having a crisis of faith.*

"Sabina, I was wondering what happened to people who practice the old ways."

"Same thing," the woman replied matter-of-factly. "We are all people in the way of the newest religion, government, or what comes down the road. No place for differences. Everyone has to be the same. Is that the practice where you come from?"

Just before falling asleep, she had wondered the same thing. "I thought it was, but not as bad here. Being different or practicing the old ways might keep me from getting a date I might want or hanging out with the popular kids, but I doubt our house would get burned down."

Sabina regarded her oddly. "What is a date or hanging out? Why are these things important?"

Good question. How did she explain dating, especially if these people participated in the practice of arranged marriages? She searched for a way to explain, but a beeping interrupted her explanation.

Leah blinked. Dawn's light peeked through her blinds, dappling her walls. Theodora meowed in her ear, reminding her breakfast, at least hers, was eminent. A loud trio of knocks rattled her door.

Ethan yelled, "Are you awake? Mom said to make sure you were awake so you wouldn't be late to school."

"I'm awake! I'm awake." She gently pushed Theo off her chest to sit up. Placing her bare feet on the floor, she cataloged everything familiar. Yes, she was home. The woods were just a dream.

www.ingramcontent.com/pod-product-compliance
Lightning Source LLC
Chambersburg PA
CBHW060427180626
46817CB00007B/2704